Alchemy

By

H. Stanley Redgrove B. Sc

Published by Forgotten Books 2012

Originally Published 1911

PIBN 1000000652

ALCHEMY:
ANCIENT AND MODERN

BEING A BRIEF ACCOUNT OF THE ALCHEMISTIC DOC-
TRINES, AND THEIR RELATIONS, TO MYSTICISM ON
THE ONE HAND, AND TO RECENT DISCOVERIES IN
PHYSICAL SCIENCE ON THE OTHER HAND; TOGETHER
WITH SOME PARTICULARS REGARDING THE LIVES
AND TEACHINGS OF THE MOST NOTED ALCHEMISTS

BY

H. STANLEY REDGROVE, B.Sc. (Lond.), F.C.S.

AUTHOR OF " ON THE CALCULATION OF THERMO-CHEMICAL CONSTANTS,"
" MATTER, SPIRIT AND THE COSMOS," ETC.

WITH 16 FULL-PAGE ILLUSTRATIONS

PHILADELPHIA
DAVID McKAY, PUBLISHER,
604-8 SOUTH WASHINGTON SQUARE.

PREFACE

THE number of books in the English language dealing with the interesting subject of Alchemy is not sufficiently great to render an apology necessary for adding thereto. Indeed, at the present time there is an actual need for a further contribution on this subject. The time is gone when it was regarded as perfectly legitimate to point to Alchemy as an instance of the aberrations of the human mind Recent experimental research has brought about profound modifications in the scientific notions regarding the chemical elements, and, indeed, in the scientific concept of the physical universe itself; and a certain resemblance can be traced between these later views and the theories of bygone Alchemy. The spontaneous change of one "element" into another has been witnessed, and the recent work of Sir William Ramsay suggests the possibility of realising the old alchemistic dream—the transmutation of the "base" metals into gold.

The basic idea permeating all the alchemistic theories appears to have been this: All the metals (and, indeed, all forms of matter) are one in origin, and are produced by an evolutionary process. The Soul of them all is one and the same; it is only the

Soul that is permanent; the body or outward form, *i.e.*, the mode of manifestation of the Soul, is transitory, and one form may be transmuted into another. The similarity, indeed it might be said, the identity, between this view and the modern etheric theory of matter is at once apparent.

The old alchemists reached the above conclusion by a theoretical method, and attempted to demonstrate the validity of their theory by means of experiment; in which, it appears, they failed. Modern science, adopting the reverse process, for a time lost hold of the idea of the unity of the physical universe, to gain it once again by the experimental method. It was in the elaboration of this grand fundamental idea that Alchemy failed. If we were asked to contrast Alchemy with the chemical and physical science of the nineteenth century we would say that, whereas the latter abounded in a wealth of much accurate detail and much relative truth, it lacked philosophical depth and insight; whilst Alchemy, deficient in such accurate detail, was characterised by a greater degree of philosophical depth and insight; for the alchemists did grasp the fundamental truth of the Cosmos, although they distorted it and made it appear grotesque. The alchemists cast their theories in a mould entirely fantastic, even ridiculous —they drew unwarrantable analogies—and hence their views cannot be accepted in these days of modern science. But if we cannot approve of their theories *in toto*, we can nevertheless appreciate the fundamental ideas at the root of them. And it is primarily with the object of pointing out this similarity between these ancient ideas regarding the physical universe and the latest products of scientific thought, that this book has been written.

It is a regrettable fact that the majority of works dealing with the subject of Alchemy take a one-sided point of view. The chemists generally take a purely physical view of the subject, and instead of trying to understand its mystical language, often (we do not say always) prefer to label it nonsense and the alchemist a fool. On the other hand, the mystics, in many cases, take a purely transcendental view of the subject, forgetting the fact that the alchemists were, for the most part, concerned with operations of a physical nature. For a proper understanding of Alchemy, as we hope to make plain in the first chapter of this work, a synthesis of both points of view is essential ; and, since these two aspects are so intimately and essentially connected with one another, this is necessary even when, as in the following work, one is concerned primarily with the physical, rather than the purely mystical, aspect of the subject.

Now, the author of this book may lay claim to being a humble student of both Chemistry and what may be generalised under the terms Mysticism and Transcendentalism ; and he hopes that this perhaps rather unusual combination of studies has enabled him to take a broad-minded view of the theories of the alchemists, and to adopt a sympathetic attitude towards them.

With regard to the illustrations, the author must express his thanks to the authorities of the British Museum for permission to photograph portrait-engravings and illustrations from old works in the

British Museum Collections, and to G. H. Gabb Esq., F.C.S., for permission to photograph portrait engravings in his possession.

The author's heartiest thanks are also due to Frank E. Weston, Esq., B.Sc., F.C.S., and W. G Llewellyn, Esq., for their kind help in reading the proofs, &c.

H. S. R.

THE POLYTECHNIC, LONDON, W.
        October, 1910.

CONTENTS

CONTENTS

CONTENTS

LIST OF PLATES

LIST OF PLATES

ALCHEMY:
ANCIENT AND MODERN

CHAPTER I

THE MEANING OF ALCHEMY

§ **1.** Alchemy is generally understood to have been that art whose end was the transmutation of the so-called base metals into gold by means of an ill-defined something called the Philosopher's Stone ; but even from a purely physical standpoint, this is a somewhat superficial view. Alchemy was both a philosophy and an experimental science, and the transmutation of the metals was its end only in that this would give the final proof of the alchemistic hypotheses ; in other words, Alchemy, considered from the physical standpoint, was the attempt to demonstrate experimentally on the material plane the validity of a certain philosophical view of the Cosmos. We see the genuine scientific spirit in the saying of one of the alchemists : " Would to God . . . all men might become adepts in our Art—for then gold, the great idol of mankind, would lose its value, and we should prize it only

The aim of Alchemy.

2

for its scientific teaching."[1]   Unfortunately, however, not many alchemists came up to this ideal; and for the majority of them, Alchemy did mean merely the possibility of making gold cheaply and gaining untold wealth.

§ 2. By some mystics, however, the opinion has been expressed that Alchemy was not a physical art or science at all, that in no sense was its object the manufacture of material gold, and that its processes were not carried out on the physical plane.   According to this transcendental theory, Alchemy was concerned with man's soul, its object was the perfection, not of material substances, but of man in a spiritual sense. Those who hold this view identify Alchemy with, or at least regard it as a branch of, Mysticism, from which it is supposed to differ merely by the employment of a special language ; and they hold that the writings of the alchemists must not be understood literally as dealing with chemical operations, with furnaces, retorts, alembics, pelicans and the like, with salt, sulphur, mercury, gold and other material substances, but must be understood as grand allegories dealing with spiritual truths.   According to this view, the figure of the transmutation of the "base" metals into gold symbolised the salvation of man—the transmutation of his soul into spiritual gold—which was to be obtained by the elimination of evil and the development of good by the grace of God; and the realisation of which salvation or spiritual trans-

The Transcendental
Theory
c emy.

_____

[1] "Eirenæus Philalethes": *An Open Entrance to the Closed Palace of the King* (see *The Hermetic Museum, Restored and Enlarged*, edited by A. E. Waite, 1893, vol. ii. p. 178).

mutation may be described as the New Birth, or that condition of being known as union with the Divine. It would follow, of course, if this theory were true, that the genuine alchemists were pure mystics, and hence, that the development of chemical science was not due to their labours, but to pseudo-alchemists who so far misunderstood their writings as to have interpreted them in a literal sense.

§ 3. This theory, however, has been effectively disposed of by Mr. Arthur Edward Waite, who **Failure of the Transcendental Theory.** points to the lives of the alchemists themselves in refutation of it. For their lives indisputably prove that the alchemists were occupied with chemical operations on the physical plane, and that for whatever motive, they toiled to discover a method for transmuting the commoner metals into actual, material gold. As Paracelsus himself says of the true " spagyric physicians," who were the alchemists of his period : "These do not give themselves up to ease and idleness . . . But they devote themselves diligently to their labours, sweating whole nights over fiery furnaces. These do not kill the time with empty talk, but find their delight in their laboratory."[2] The writings of the alchemists contain (mixed, however, with much that from the physical standpoint appears merely fantastic) accurate accounts of many chemical processes and discoveries, which cannot be explained away by any method of transcendental interpretation. There is not the slightest doubt that chemistry owes its origin

[2] PARACELSUS : "Concerning the Nature of Things " (see *The Hermetic and Alchemical Writings of Paracelsus*, edited by A. E. Waite, 1894, vol. i. p. 167).

to the direct labours of the alchemists themselves, and not to any who misread their writings.

§ 4. At the same time, it is quite evident that there is a considerable element of Mysticism in the alchemistic doctrines ; this has always been recognised ; but, as a general rule, those who have approached the subject from the scientific point of view have considered this mystical element as of little or no importance. However, there are certain curious facts which are not satisfactorily explained by a purely physical theory of Alchemy, and, in our opinion, the recognition of the importance of this mystical element and of the true relation which existed between Alchemy and Mysticism is essential for the right understanding of the subject. We may notice, in the first place, that the alchemists always speak of their Art as a Divine Gift, the highest secrets of which are not to be learnt from any books on the subject ; and they invariably teach that the right mental attitude with regard to God is the first step necessary for the achievement of the *magnum opus*. As says one alchemist : "In the first place, let every devout and God-fearing chemist and student of this Art consider that this arcanum should be regarded, not only as a truly great, but as a most holy Art (seeing that it typifies and shadows out the highest heavenly good). Therefore, if any man desire to reach this great and unspeakable Mystery, he must remember that it is obtained not by the might of man, but by the grace of God, and that not our will or desire, but only the mercy of the Most High, can bestow it upon us. For this reason you must first of all cleanse your

The Qualifications of the Adept.

heart, lift it up to Him alone, and ask of Him this gift in true, earnest, and undoubting prayer. He alone can give and bestow it."[3]   And " Basil Valentine " : " First, there should be the invocation of God, flowing from the depth of a pure and sincere heart, and a conscience which should be free from all ambition, hypocrisy, and vice, as also from all cognate faults, such as arrogance, boldness, pride, luxury, worldly vanity, oppression of the poor, and similar iniquities, which should all be rooted up out of the heart—that when a man appears before the Throne of Grace, to regain the health of his body, he may come with a conscience weeded of all tares, and be changed into a pure temple of God cleansed of all that defiles."[4]

§ **5.** In the second place, we must notice the nature of alchemistic language. As we have hinted above, and as is at once apparent on opening any alchemistic book, the language of Alchemy is very highly mystical, and there is much that is perfectly unintelligible in a physical sense. Indeed, the alchemists habitually apologise for their vagueness on the plea that such mighty secrets may not be made more fully manifest. It is true, of course, that in the days of Alchemy s degeneracy a good deal of pseudo-mystical nonsense was written by the many impostors then abounding, but the mystical style of language is by no means confined to the later alchemistic writings. It is also

Alchemistic Language

---

[3] *The Sophic Hydrolith ; or, Water Stone of the Wise* (see *The Hermetic Museum,* vol. i. p. 74).

[4] *The Triumphal Chariot of Antimony* (Mr. A. E. Waite's translation, p. 13).   See § 41.

true that the alchemists, no doubt, desired to shield their secrets from vulgar and profane eyes, and hence would necessarily adopt a symbolic language. But it is past belief that the language of the alchemist was due to some arbitrary plan ; whatever it is to us, it was very real to him. Moreover, this argument cuts both ways, for those, also, who take a transcendental view of Alchemy regard its language as symbolical, although after a different manner. It is also, to say the least, curious, as Mr. A. E. Waite points out, that this mystical element should be found in the writings of the earlier alchemists, whose manuscripts were not written for publication, and therefore ran no risk of informing the vulgar of the precious secrets of Alchemy. On the other hand, the transcendental method of translation does often succeed in making sense out of what is otherwise unintelligible in the writings of the alchemists. The above-mentioned writer remarks on this point : " Without in any way pretending to assert that this hypothesis reduces the literary chaos of the philosophers into a regular order, it may be affirmed that it materially elucidates their writings, and that it is wonderful how contradictions, absurdities, and difficulties seem to dissolve wherever it is applied."[5]

The alchemists' love of symbolism is also conspicuously displayed in the curious designs with which certain of their books are embellished. We are not here referring to the illustrations of actual apparatus employed in carrying out the various operations of physical Alchemy, which are not infrequently found in the works of those alchemists who at the same time

[5] ARTHUR EDWARD WAITE : *The Occult Sciences* (1891), p. 91.

were practical chemists (Glauber, for example), but to pictures whose meaning plainly lies not upon the surface and whose import is clearly symbolical, whether their symbolism has reference to physical or to spiritual processes. Examples of such symbolic illustrations, many of which are highly fantastic, will be found in plates 2, 3, and 4. We shall refer to them again in the course of the present and following chapters.

§ **6**. We must also notice that, although there cannot be the slightest doubt that the great majority of alchemists were engaged in problems and experiments of a physical nature, yet there were a few men included within the alchemistic ranks who were entirely, or almost entirely, concerned with problems of a spiritual nature ; Thomas Vaughan, for example, and Jacob Boehme, who boldly employed the language of Alchemy in the elaboration of his system of mystical philosophy. And particularly must we notice, as Mr. A. E. Waite has also indicated, the significant fact that the Western alchemists make unanimous appeal to Hermes Trismegistos as the greatest authority on the art of Alchemy, whose alleged writings are of an undoubtedly mystical character (see § 29). It is clear, that in spite of its apparently physical nature, Alchemy must have been in some way closely connected with Mysticism.

Alchemists of a Mystical Type.

§ **7**. If we are ever to understand the meaning of Alchemy aright we must look at the subject from the alchemistic point of view. In modern times there has come about a divorce between Religion and Science in men's minds (though more recently a uni-

fying tendency has set in); but it was otherwise with
the alchemists, their religion and their science were
closely united. We have said that
"Alchemy was the attempt to demonstrate experimentally on the material
plane the validity of a certain philosophical view of
the Cosmos"; now, this "philosophical view of the
Cosmos" was Mysticism. **Alchemy had its origin
in the attempt to apply, in a certain manner, the
principles of Mysticism to the things of the physical
plane,** and was, therefore, of a dual nature, on the one
hand spiritual and religious, on the other, physical
and material. As the anonymous author of *Lives of
Alchemystical Philosophers* (1815) remarks, "The
universal chemistry, by which the science of alchemy
opens the knowledge of all nature, being founded on
first principles forms analogy with whatever knowledge is founded on the *same first principles*. . . .
Saint John describes the redemption, or the new
creation of the fallen soul, on the *same first principles*,
until the consummation of the work, in which the
Divine tincture transmutes the base metal of the soul
into a perfection, that will pass the fire of eternity;"[6]
that is to say, Alchemy and the mystical regeneration
of man (in this writer's opinion) are analogous processes on different planes of being, because they are
founded on the same first principles.

§ **8.** We shall here quote the opinions of two
modern writers, as to the significance of Alchemy;
one a mystic, the other a man of science. Says Mr.
A. E. Waite, "If the authors of the 'Suggestive
Inquiry' and of 'Remarks on Alchemy and the

[6] F. B. : *Lives of Alchemystical Philosophers* (1815), Preface, p. 3.

Alchemists' [two books putting forward the transcendental theory] had considered the lives of the sym-
bolists, as well as the nature of the
symbols, their views would have been very
much modified; they would have found
that the true method of Hermetic interpretation lies
in a middle course; but the errors which originated
with merely typographical investigations were inten-
sified by a consideration of the great alchemical
theorem, which, *par excellence*, is one of universal
development, which acknowledges that every substance contains undeveloped resources and poten-
tialities, and can be brought outward and forward
into perfection. They [the generality of alchemists]
applied their theory only to the development of
metallic substances from a lower to a higher order,
but we see by their writings that the grand
hierophants of Oriental and Western alchemy alike
were continually haunted by brief and imperfect
glimpses of glorious possibilities for man, if the evolution of his nature were accomplished along the lines of
their theory."[7] Mr. M. M. Pattison Muir, M.A.,

(marginal note) other Writers.

[7] ARTHUR EDWARD WAITE: *Lives of Alchemystical Philosophers*
(1888), pp. 30, 31. As says another writer of the mystical school of
thought : " If we look upon the subject [of Alchymy] from the point
which affords the widest view, it may be said that Alchymy has two
aspects : the simply material, and the religious. The dogma that
Alchymy was only a form of chemistry is untenable by any one who
has read the works of its chief professors. The doctrine that
Alchymy was religion only, and that its chemical references were all
blinds, is equally untenable in the face of history, which shows that
many of its most noted professors were men who had made important
discoveries in the domain of common chemistry, and were in no way
notable as teachers either of ethics or religion " (" Sapere Aude," *The
Science of Alchymy, Spiritual and Material* (1893), pp. 3 and 4).

says : ". . . alchemy aimed at giving experimental proof of a certain theory of the whole system of nature, including humanity. The practical culmination of the alchemical quest presented a threefold aspect ; the alchemists sought the stone of wisdom, for by gaining that they gained the control of wealth ; they sought the universal panacea, for that would give them the power of enjoying wealth and life ; they sought the soul of the world, for thereby they could hold communion with spiritual existences, and enjoy the fruition of spiritual life. The object of their search was to satisfy their material needs, their intellectual capacities, and their spiritual yearnings. The alchemists of the nobler sort always made the first of these objects subsidiary to the other two. . . ." [8]

§ 9. The famous axiom beloved by every alchemist —" *What is above is as that which is below, and what is below is as that which is above*"—although of questable origin, tersely expresses the basic

T Ba: ea
of Alchemy

idea of Alchemy. The alchemists postulated and believed in a very real sense in the essential unity of the Cosmos. Hence, they held that there is a correspondence or analogy existing between things spiritual and things physical, the same laws operating in each realm. As writes Sendivogius ". . . the Sages have been taught of God that this natural world is only an image and material copy of a heavenly and spiritual pattern ; that the very existence of this world is based upon the reality of its celestial archetype ; and that God has created it in imitation of the spiritual and invisible universe, in order that men

[8] M. M. PATTISON MUIR, M.A. : *The Story of Alchemy and the Beginnings of Chemistry* (1902), pp. 105 and 106.

might be the better enabled to comprehend His heavenly teaching, and the wonders of His absolute and ineffable power and wisdom. Thus the Sage sees heaven reflected in Nature as in a mirror; and he pursues this Art, not for the sake of gold or silver, but for the love of the knowledge which it reveals; he jealously conceals it from the sinner and the scornful, lest the mysteries of heaven should be laid bare to the vulgar gaze." [9]

The alchemists held that the metals are one in essence, and spring from the same seed in the womb of nature, but are not all equally matured and perfect, gold being the highest product of Nature's powers. In gold, the alchemist saw a picture of the regenerate man, resplendent with spiritual beauty, overcoming all temptations and proof against evil; whilst he regarded lead—the basest of the metals—as typical of the sinful and unregenerate man, stamped with the hideousness of sin and easily overcome by temptation and evil; for whilst gold withstood the action of fire and all known corrosive liquids (save *aqua regia* alone), lead was most easily acted upon. We are told that the Philosopher's Stone, which would bring about the desired grand transmutation, is of a species with gold itself and purer than the purest; understood in the mystical sense this means that the regeneration of man can be effected only by Goodness itself—in terms of Christian theology, by the Power of the Spirit of Christ. The Philosopher's Stone was regarded as symbolical of Christ Jesus, and in this sense we can understand the otherwise incredible powers attributed to it.

[9] MICHAEL SENDIVOGIUS : *The New Chemical Light, Pt. II., Concerning Sulphur* (*The Hermetic Museum*, vol. ii. p. 138).

§ **10.** With the theories of physical Alchemy we shall deal at length in the following chapter, but

The Law of Analogy.

enough has been said to indicate the analogy existing, according to the alchemistic view, between the problem of the perfection of the metals, *i.e.*, the transmutation of the "base" metals into gold, and the perfection or transfiguration of spiritual man ; and it might also be added, between these problems and that of the perfection of man considered physiologically. To the alchemistic philosopher these three problems were one : the same problem on different planes of being ; and the solution was likewise one. He who held the key to one problem held the key to all three, provided he understood the analogy between matter and spirit. The point is not, be it noted, whether these problems are in reality one and the same ; the main doctrine of analogy, which is, indeed, an essential element in all true mystical philosophy, will, we suppose, meet with general consent ; but it will be contended (and rightly, we think) that the analogies drawn by the alchemists are fantastic and by no means always correct, though possibly there may be more truth in them than appears at first sight. The point is not that these analogies are correct, but that they were regarded as such by all true alchemists. Says the author of *The Sophic Hydrolith:* ". . . the practice of this Art enables us to understand, not merely the marvels of Nature, but the nature of God Himself, in all its unspeakable glory. It shadows forth, in a wonderful manner . . . all the articles of the Christian faith, and the reason why man must pass through much tribulation and anguish, and fall a prey to death, before he can rise again to a new life." [10]   A considerable portion of this curious alchemistic work is taken up in expounding the analogy believed to exist between the Philosopher's Stone and "the Stone which the builders rejected," Christ Jesus ; and the writer concludes : "Thus . . . I have briefly and simply set forth to you the perfect analogy which exists between our earthly and chemical and the true and heavenly Stone, Jesus Christ, whereby we may attain unto certain beatitude and perfection, not only in earthly but also in eternal life." [11]   And likewise says Peter Bonus : "I am firmly persuaded that any unbeliever who got truly to know this Art, would straightway confess the truth of our Blessed Religion, and believe in the Trinity and in our Lord Jesus Christ." [12]

§ 11. For the most part, the alchemists were chiefly engaged with the carrying out of the alchemistic theory on the physical plane, i.e., with the attempt to transmute the "base" metals into the "noble" ones ; some for the love of knowledge, but alas! the vast majority for the love of mere wealth.   But all who were worthy of the title of "alchemist" realised at times, more or less dimly, the possibility of the application of the same methods to man and the glorious result of the transmutation of man's soul into spiritual gold.   There were a few who had a

The Dual Nature of Alchemy.

---

[10] *The Sophic Hydrolith ; or, Water Stone of the Wise* (see *The Hermetic Museum*, vol. i. p. 88).

[11] *Ibid.* p. 114.

[12] PETER BONUS : *The New Pearl of Great Price* (Mr. A. E. Waite's translation, p. 275).

clearer vision of this ideal, those who devoted their activities entirely, or almost so, to the attainment of this highest goal of alchemistic philosophy, and concerned themselves little if at all with the analogous problem on the physical plane. The theory that Alchemy originated in the attempt to demonstrate the applicability of the principles of Mysticism to the things of the physical realm brings into harmony the physical and transcendental theories of Alchemy and the various conflicting facts advanced in favour of each. It explains the existence of the above-mentioned, two very different types of alchemists. It explains the appeal to the works attributed to Hermes, and the presence in the writings of the alchemists of much that is clearly mystical. And finally, it is in agreement with such statements as we have quoted above from *The Sophic Hydrolith* and elsewhere, and the general religious tone of the alchemistic writings.

§ **12.** In accordance with our primary object as stated in the preface, we shall confine our attention mainly to the physical aspect of Alchemy; but in order to understand its theories, it appears to us to be essential to realise the fact that Alchemy was an attempted application of the principles of Mysticism to the things of the physical world. The supposed analogy between man and the metals sheds light on what otherwise would be very difficult to understand. It helps to make plain why the alchemists attributed moral qualities to the metals—some are called " imperfect," " base "; others are said to be " perfect," " noble." And especially does it help to explain the alchemistic

PLATE 2.

SYMBOLICAL ILLUSTRATION
Representing the
Trinity of Body, Soul and Spirit.

notions regarding the nature of the metals. The alchemists believed that the metals were constructed after the manner of man, into whose constitution three factors were regarded as entering : body, soul, and spirit. As regards man, mystical philosophers generally use these terms as follows : " body " is the outward manifestation and form ; "soul" is the inward individual spirit [13] ; and "spirit" is the universal Soul in all men. And likewise, according to the alchemists, in the metals, there is the "body" or outward form and properties, "metalline soul" or spirit,[14] and finally, the all-pervading essence of all metals. As writes Nicholas Barnaud, in his exceedingly curious tract entitled *The Book of Lambspring :* " Be warned and understand truly that two fishes are swimming in our sea," illustrating his remark by the symbolical picture reproduced in plate 2, and adding in elucidation thereof, " The Sea is the Body, the two Fishes are Soul and Spirit." [15] The alchemists, however, were not always consistent in their use of the term "spirit." Sometimes (indeed frequently) they employed it to denote merely the more volatile portions of a chemical substance ; at other times it had a more interior significance.

§ **13.** We notice the great difference between the

[13] Which, in virtue of man's self-consciousness, is, by the grace of God, immortal.

[14] See the work *Of Natural and Supernatural Things*, attributed to " Basil Valentine," for a description of the "spirits" of the metals in particular.

[15] NICHOLAS BARNAUD DELPHINAS: *The Book of Lambspring* (see the *Hermetic Museum*, vol. i. p. 277). This work contains many other fantastic alchemistic symbolical pictures, probably the most curious series in all alchemistic literature

alchemistic theory and the views regarding the constitution of matter which have dominated Chemistry

Al 'iemv
Mysticism
and Modern
science.
since the time of Dalton.   But at the
present time Dalton's theory of the
chemical elements is undergoing a profound modification.   We do not imply
that Modern Science is going back to any such fantastic ideas as were held by the alchemists, but we
are struck with the remarkable similarity between
this alchemistic theory of a soul of all metals, a
one primal element, and modern views regarding
the ether of space.   In its attempt to demonstrate
the applicability of the fundamental principles of Mysticism to the things of the physical realm Alchemy
apparently failed and ended its days in fraud.   It
appears, however, that this true aim of alchemistic
art—particularly the demonstration of the validity of
the theory that all the various forms of matter are
produced by an evolutionary process from some one
primal element or *quintessence*—is being realised by
recent researches in the domain of physical and
chemical science.

CHAPTER II

THE THEORY OF PHYSICAL ALCHEMY

§ **14.** It must be borne in mind when reviewing the theories of the alchemists, that there were a number

Supposed Proofs of Trans-mutation.

of phenomena known at the time, the superficial examination of which would naturally engender a belief that the transmutation of the metals was a common occurrence. For example, the deposition of copper on iron when immersed in a solution of a copper salt (*e.g.*, blue vitriol) was naturally concluded to be a transmutation of iron into copper,[1] although, had the alchemists examined the residual liquid, they would have found that the two metals had merely exchanged places; and the fact that white and yellow alloys of copper with arsenic and other substances could be produced, pointed to the possibility of transmuting copper into silver and gold. It was also known that if water (and this is true of distilled water which does not contain solid matter in solution) was boiled for some time in a glass flask, some solid, earthy matter was produced ; and if water could be transmuted into earth, surely one metal could be

[1] Cf. *The Golden Tract concerning the Stone of the Philosophers* (*The Hermetic Museum*, vol. i. p. 25).

converted into another.[2] On account of these and like phenomena the alchemists regarded the transmutation of the metals as an experimentally proved fact. Even if they are to be blamed for their superficial observation of such phenomena, yet, nevertheless, their labours marked a distinct advance upon the purely speculative and theoretical methods of the philosophers preceding them. Whatever their faults, the alchemists *were* the forerunners of modern experimental science.

§ **15.** The alchemists regarded the metals as composite, and granting this, then the possibility of transmutation is only a logical conclusion. In order to understand the theory of the elements held by them we must rid ourselves of any idea that it bears any close resemblance to Dalton's theory of the chemical elements ; this is clear from what has been said in the preceding chapter. Now, it is a fact of simple observation that many otherwise different bodies manifest some property in common, as, for instance, combustibility. Properties such as these were regarded as being due to some principle or element common to all bodies exhibiting such properties ; thus, combustibility was thought to be due to some elementary principle of combustion—the " sulphur " of the alchemists and the " phlogiston " of a later period. This is a view which *a priori* appears to be not unlikely ; but it is now known that, although there are relations existing between the properties of bodies

The Alchemistic Elements.

---

[2] Lavoisier (eighteenth century) proved this apparent transmutation to be due to the action of the water on the glass vessel containing it.

and their constituent chemical elements (and also, it should be noted, the relative arrangement of the particles of these elements), it is the less obvious properties which enable chemists to determine the constitution of bodies, and the connection is very far from being of the simple nature imagined by the alchemists.

§ **16.** For the origin of the alchemistic theory of the elements it is necessary to go back to the philosophers

Aristotle's Views regarding the Elements.

preceding the alchemists, and it is not improbable that they derived it from some still older source. It was taught by Empedocles of Agrigent (440 B.C. *circa*), who considered that there were four elements— earth, water, air, and fire. Aristotle added a fifth, "the ether." These elements were regarded, not as different kinds of matter, but rather as different forms of the one original matter, whereby it manifested different properties. It was thought that to these elements were due the four primary properties of dryness, moistness, warmth, and coldness, each element being supposed to give rise to two of these properties, dryness and warmth being thought to be due to fire, moistness and warmth to air, moistness and coldness to water, and dryness and coldness to earth. Thus, moist and cold bodies (liquids in general) were said to possess these properties in consequence of the aqueous element, and were termed "waters," &c. Also, since these elements were not regarded as different kinds of matter, transmutation was thought to be possible, one being convertible into another, as in the example given above (§ 14).

§ **17.** Coming to the alchemists, we find the view that the metals are all composed of two elementary principles—sulphur and mercury—in different proportions and degrees of purity, well-nigh universally accepted in the earlier days of Alchemy. By these terms "sulphur" and "mercury," however, must not be understood the common bodies ordinarily designated by these names ; like the elements of Aristotle, the alchemistic principles were regarded as properties rather than as substances, though it must be confessed that the alchemists were by no means always clear on this point themselves. Indeed, it is not altogether easy to say exactly what the alchemists did mean by these terms, and the question is complicated by the fact that very frequently they make mention of different sorts of "sulphur" and "mercury." Probably, however, we shall not be far wrong in saying that "sulphur" was generally regarded as the principle of combustion and also of colour, and was said to be present on account of the fact that most metals are changed into earthy substances by the aid of fire ; and to the " mercury," the metallic principle *par excellence*, was attributed such properties as fusibility, malleability and lustre, which were regarded as characteristic of the metals in general. The pseudo-Geber (see § 32) says that " Sulphur is a fatness of the Earth, by temperate Decoction in the Mine of the Earth thickened, until it be hardned and made dry." [3]   He considered an excess of sulphur to be a cause of imperfection in the metals, and he writes

The Sulphur-Mercury Theory.

---

[3] *Of the Sum of Perfection* (see *The Works of Geber*, translated by Richard Russel, 1678, pp. 69 and 70).

that one of the causes of the corruption of the metals by fire " is the Inclusion of a burning Sulphuriety in the profundity of their Substance, diminishing them by Inflamation, and exterminating also into Fume, with extream Consumption, whatsoever Argentvive in them is of good Fixation." [4]   He assumed, further, that the metals contained an incombustible as well as a combustible sulphur, the latter sulphur being apparently regarded as an impurity.[5]   A later alchemist says that sulphur is "most easily recognised by the vital spirit in animals, the colour in metals, the odour in plants."[6]   Mercury, on the other hand, according to the pseudo-Geber, is the cause of perfection in the metals, and endows gold with its lustre.   Another alchemist, quoting Arnold de Villanova, writes : " Quicksilver is the elementary form of all things fusible ; for all things fusible, when melted, are changed into it, and it mingles with them because it is of the same substance with them.   Such bodies differ from quicksilver in their composition only so far as itself is or is not free from the foreign matter of impure sulphur." [7]   The obtaining of "philosophical mercury," the imaginary virtues of which the alchemists never tired of relating, was generally held to be essential for the attainment of the *magnum opus*.   It was commonly thought that it could be prepared from ordinary quicksilver by

---

[4] *Of the Sum of Perfection* (see *The Works of Geber*, p. 156).

[5] See *The Works of Geber*, p. 160.   This view was also held by other alchemists.

[6] *The New Chemical Light*, Part II., *Concerning Sulphur* (see *The Hermetic Museum*, vol. ii. p. 151).

[7] See *The Golden Tract concerning the Stone of the Philosophers* (*The Hermetic Museum*, vol. i. p. 17).

purificatory processes, whereby the impure sulphur supposed to be present in this sort of mercury might be purged away.

The sulphur-mercury theory of the metals was held by such famous alchemists as Roger Bacon, Arnold de Villanova and Raymond Lully.   Until recently it was thought to have originated to a great extent with the Arabian alchemist, Geber ; but the late Professor Berthelot showed that the works ascribed to Geber, in which the theory is put forward, are forgeries of a date by which it was already centuries old (see § 32). Occasionally, arsenic was regarded as an elementary principle (this view is to be found, for example, in the work *Of the Sum of Perfection*, by the pseudo-Geber), but the idea was not general.

§ **18.** Later in the history of Alchemy, the mercury-sulphur theory was extended by the addition of a third elementary principle, salt. As in **The Sulphur-Mercury-Salt Theory** the case of philosophical sulphur and mercury, by this term was not meant common salt (sodium chloride) or any of those substances commonly known as salts. "Salt" was the name given to a supposed basic principle in the metals, a principle of fixity and solidification, conferring the property of resistance to fire. In this extended form, the theory is found in the works of Isaac of Holland and in those attributed to " Basil Valentine," who (see the work *Of Natural and Supernatural Things*) attempts to explain the differences in the properties of the metals as the result of the differences in the proportion of sulphur, salt, and mercury they contain. Thus, copper, which is highly coloured, is said to contain much sulphur, whilst iron

is supposed to contain an excess of salt, &c. The
sulphur-mercury-salt theory was vigorously cham-
pioned by Paracelsus, and the doctrine gained very
general acceptance amongst the alchemists. Salt,
however, seems generally to have been considered
a less important principle than either mercury or
sulphur.

The same germ-idea underlying these doctrines
is to be found much later in Stahl's phlogistic
theory (eighteenth century), which attempted to
account for the combustibility of bodies by the
assumption that such bodies all contain "phlogiston"
—the hypothetical principle of combustion (see § 72)—
though the concept of "phlogiston" approaches more
nearly to the modern idea of an element than do the
alchemistic elements or principles. It was not until
still later in the history of Chemistry that it became
quite evident that the more obvious properties of
chemical substances are not specially conferred on
them in virtue of certain elements entering into their
constitution.

§ **19.** The alchemists combined the above theories
with Aristotle's theory of the elements. The latter,
namely, earth, air, fire and water, were
Alchemistic Elements and Principles. regarded as more interior, more primary,
than the principles, whose source was
said to be these same elements. As
writes Sendivogius in Part II. of *The New Chemical
Light*: "The three Principles of things are produced
out of the four elements in the following manner:
Nature, whose power is in her obedience to the Will
of God, ordained from the very beginning, that the
four elements should incessantly act on one another,

so, in obedience to her behest, fire began to act on air, and produced Sulphur ; air acted on water, and produced Mercury ; water, by its action on the earth, produced Salt. Earth, alone, having nothing to act upon, did not produce anything, but became the nurse, or womb, of these three Principles. We designedly speak of three Principles ; for though the Ancients mention only two, it is clear that they omitted the third (Salt) not from ignorance, but from a desire to lead the uninitiated astray." [8]

Beneath and within all these coverings of outward properties, taught the alchemists, is hidden the secret essence of all material things. " . . . the elements and compounds," writes one alchemist, " in addition to crass matter, are composed of a subtle substance, or intrinsic radical humidity, diffused through the elemental parts, simple and wholly incorruptible, long preserving the things themselves in vigour, and called the Spirit of the World, proceeding from the Soul of the World, the one certain life, filling and fathoming all things, gathering together and connecting all things, so that from the three genera of creatures, Intellectual, Celestial, and Corruptible, there is formed the One Machine of the whole world." [9] It is hardly necessary to point out how nearly this approaches modern views regarding the Ether of Space.

[8] *The New Chemical Light*, Part II., *Concerning Sulphur* (see *The Hermetic Museum*, vol. ii. pp. 142–143).

[9] ALEXANDER VON SUCHTEN : *Man, the best and most perfect of God's creatures. A more complete Exposition of this Medical Foundation for the less Experienced Student.* (See BENEDICTUS FIGULUS : *A Golden and Blessed Casket of Nature's Marvels*, translated by A. E. Waite, 1893, pp. 71 and 72.)

§ **20**. The alchemists regarded the metals as growing in the womb of the earth, and a knowledge of this growth as being of very great importance. Thomas Norton (who, however, contrary to the generality of alchemists, denied that metals have seed and that they grow in the sense of multiply) says :—

The G   h of
the Metals

> " *Mettalls* of kinde grow lowe under ground,
> For above erth rust in them is found ;
> Soe above erth appeareth corruption,
> Of mettalls, and in long tyme destruction,
> Whereof noe Cause is found in this Case,
> Buth that above Erth thei be not in their place
> Contrarie places to nature causeth strife
> As Fishes out of water losen their Lyfe :
> And Man, with Beasts, and Birds live in ayer,
> But Stones and Mineralls under Erth repaier." [10]

Norton here expresses the opinion, current among the alchemists, that each and every thing has its own peculiar environment natural to it ; a view controverted by Robert Boyle (§ 71). So firm was the belief in the growth of metals, that mines were frequently closed for a while in order that the supply of metal might be renewed. The fertility of Mother Earth forms the subject of one of the illustrations in *The Twelve Keys* of " Basil Valentine " (see § 41). We reproduce it in plate 3, fig. A. Regarding this subject, the author writes : " The quickening power of the earth produces all things that grow forth from it, and he who says that the earth has no life makes

---

[10] THOMAS NORTON : *Ordinall of Alchemy* (see *Theatrum Chemicum Britannicum*, edited by Elias Ashmole, 1652, p. 18).

a statement which is flatly contradicted by the most ordinary facts. For what is dead cannot produce life and growth, seeing that it is devoid of the quickening spirit. This spirit is the life and soul that dwell in the earth, and are nourished by heavenly and sidereal influences. For all herbs, trees, and roots, and all metals and minerals, receive their growth and nutriment from the spirit of the earth, which is the spirit of life. This spirit is itself fed by the stars, and is thereby rendered capable of imparting nutriment to all things that grow, and of nursing them as a mother does her child while it is yet in the womb. The minerals are hidden in the womb of the earth, and nourished by her with the spirit which she receives from above.

"Thus the power of growth that I speak of is imparted not by the earth, but by the life-giving spirit that is in it. If the earth were deserted by this spirit, it would be dead, and no longer able to afford nourishment to anything. For its sulphur or richness would lack the quickening spirit without which there can be neither life nor growth." [11]

§ 21. The idea that the growth of each metal was under the influence of one of the heavenly bodies *[and Astrology.]* (a theory in harmony with the alchemistic view of the unity of the Cosmos), was very generally held by the alchemists; and in consequence thereof, the metals were often referred to by the names or astrological symbols of their peculiar planets. These particulars are shown in the following table :—

[11] "BASIL VALENTINE": *The Twelve Keys* (see *The Hermetic Museum*, vol i. pp. 333–334).

PLATE 3

A.

SYMBOLICAL ILLUSTRATION

Representing the
Fertility of the Earth.

B

SYMBOLICAL ILLUSTRATION

Representing the
Amalgamation of Gold with Mercury.

(See page 33.)

To face page 26]

Metals.	Planets, &c.[12]	Symbols.
Gold	Sun	☉
Silver	Moon	☽
Mercury	Mercury	☿
Copper	Venus	♀
Iron	Mars	♂
Tin	Jupiter	♃
Lead	Saturn	♄

Moreover, it was thought by some alchemists that a due observance of astrological conditions was necessary for successfully carrying out important alchemistic experiments.

§ **22.** The alchemists regarded gold as the most perfect metal, silver being considered more perfect than the rest. The reason of this view is not difficult to understand : gold is the most beautiful of all the metals, and it retains its beauty without tarnishing ; it resists the action of fire and most corrosive liquids, and is unaffected by sulphur ; it was regarded, as we have pointed out above (see § 9), as symbolical of the regenerate man. Silver, on the other hand, is, indeed, a beautiful metal which wears well in a pure atmosphere and resists the action of fire ; but it is attacked by certain corrosives (*e.g.*, *aqua fortis* or nitric acid) and also by sulphur. Through all the metals, from the one seed, Nature, according to the

Alchemistic View of the Nature of Gold.

[12] This supposed connection between the metals and planets also played an important part in Talismanic Magic.

alchemists, works continuously up to gold ; so that, in
a sense, all other metals are gold in the making ; their
existence marks the staying of Nature's powers ; as
" Eirenæus Philalethes " says : " All metallic seed is
the seed of gold ; for gold is the intention of Nature in
regard to all metals. If the base metals are not gold,
it is only through some accidental hindrance ; they
are all potentially gold." [13]   Or, as another alchemist
puts it : " Since . . . the substance of the metals is
one, and common to all, and since this substance is
(either at once, or after laying aside in course of time
the foreign and evil sulphur of the baser metals by a
process of gradual digestion) changed by the virtue of
its own indwelling sulphur into GOLD, which is the
goal of all the metals, and the true intention of
Nature—we are obliged to admit, and freely confess
that in the mineral kingdom, as well as in the
vegetable and animal kingdoms, Nature seeks and
demands a gradual attainment of perfection, and a
gradual approximation to the highest standard of
purity and excellence." [14]   Such was the alchemistic
view of the generation of the metals ; a theory which
is admittedly crude, but which, nevertheless, contains
the germ of a great principle of the utmost importance,
namely, the idea that all the varying forms of matter
are evolved from some one primordial stuff—a
principle of which chemical science lost sight for
awhile ; for its validity was unrecognised by Dalton's
Atomic Theory (at least, as enunciated by him),

[13] " EIRENÆUS PHILALETHES " : *The Metamorphosis of Metals*
(see *The Hermetic Museum*, vol. ii. p. 239).
[14] *The Golden Tract Concerning the Stone of the Philosophers*
(see *The Hermetic Museum*, vol. i. p. 19).

but which is being demonstrated, as we hope to show hereinafter, by recent scientific research. The alchemist was certainly a fantastic evolutionist, but he *was* an evolutionist, and, moreover, he did not make the curious and paradoxical mistake of regarding the fact of evolution as explaining away the existence of God—the alchemist recognised the hand of the Divine in nature—and, although, in these days of modern science, we cannot accept his theory of the growth of metals, we can, nevertheless, appreciate and accept the fundamental germ-idea underlying it.

§ **23.** The alchemist strove to assist Nature in her gold-making, or, at least, to carry out her methods.

The Philosopher s Stone.

The pseudo-Geber taught that the imperfect metals were to be perfected or cured by the application of "medicines." Three forms of medicines were distinguished ; the first bring about merely a temporary change, and the changes wrought by the second class, although permanent, are not complete. "A Medicine of the third Order," he writes, "I call every Preparation, which, when it comes to Bodies, with its projection, takes away all Corruption, and perfects them with the Difference of all Compleatment. But this is one only." [15] This, the true medicine that would produce a real and permanent transmutation, is the **Philosopher's Stone,** the Masterpiece of alchemistic art. Similar views were held by all the alchemists, though some of them taught that it was necessary first of all to reduce the metals to their first

[15] *Of the Sum of Perfection* (see *The Works of Geber,* translated by Richard Russel, 1678, p. 192).

substance.   Often, two forms of the Philosopher's
Stone were distinguished, or perhaps we should say,
two degrees of perfection in the one Stone ; that for
transmuting the "imperfect" metals into silver being
said to be white, the stone or "powder of projection"
for gold being said to be of a red colour.   In other
accounts (see Chapter V.) the medicine is described
as of a pale brimstone hue.

Most of the alchemists who claimed knowledge of
the Philosopher's Stone or the *materia prima* necessary
for its preparation, generally kept its nature most
secret, and spoke only in the most enigmatical and
allegorical language, the majority of their recipes containing words of unknown meaning.   In some cases
gold or silver, as the case may be, was employed in
preparing the "medicine"; and, after projection had
been made, this was, of course, obtained again in
the metallic form, the alchemist imagining that a
transmutation had been effected.   In the case of the
few other recipes that are intelligible, the most that
could be obtained by following out their instructions
is a white or yellow metallic alloy superficially
resembling silver or gold.

§ **24.** The mystical as distinguished from the
pseudo-practical descriptions of the Stone and its
The Nature   preparation are by far the more in-
of the   teresting of the two.   Paracelsus, in his
Philosopher's   work on *The Tincture of the Philosophers*,
Stone.   tells us that all that is necessary for us to
do is to mix and coagulate the "rose-coloured blood
from the Lion" and "the gluten from the Eagle," by
which he probably meant that we must combine
"philosophical sulphur" with "philosophical mercury."

This opinion, that the Philosopher's Stone consists of " philosophical sulphur and mercury " combined so as to constitute a perfect unity, was commonly held by the alchemists, and they frequently likened this union to the conjunction of the sexes in marriage. "Eirenæus Philalethes" tells us that for the preparation of the Stone it is necessary to extract the seed of gold, though this cannot be accomplished by subjecting gold to corrosive liquids, but only by a homogeneous water (or liquid)—the Mercury of the Sages.   In the *Book of the Revelation of Hermes, interpreted by Theophrastus Paracelsus, concerning the Supreme Secret of the World*, the Medicine, which is here, as not infrequently, identified with the alchemistic essence of all things or Soul of the World, is described in the following suggestive language : " This is the Spirit of Truth, which the world cannot comprehend without the interposition of the Holy Ghost, or without the instruction of those who know it.   The same is of a mysterious nature, wondrous strength, boundless power. . . . By Avicenna this Spirit is named the Soul of the World.   For, as the Soul moves all the limbs of the Body, so also does this Spirit move all bodies.   And as the Soul is in all the limbs of the Body, so also is this Spirit in all elementary created things.   It is sought by many and found by few.   It is beheld from afar and found near ; for it exists in every thing, in every place, and at all times.   It has the powers of all creatures ; its action is found in all elements, and the qualities of all things are therein, even in the highest per- fection . . . it heals all dead and living bodies without other medicine, . . . converts all metallic

bodies into gold, and there is nothing like unto it
under Heaven." [16]

§ **25.** From the ascetic standpoint (and unfortunately, most mystics have been somewhat overfond
of ascetic ideas), the development of
The Theory the soul is only fully possible with the
of Develop-
ment. mortification of the body ; and all true
Mysticism teaches that if we would reach
the highest goal possible for man—union with the
Divine—there must be a giving up of our own individual wills, an abasement of the soul before the
Spirit. And so the alchemists taught that for the
achievement of the *magnum opus* on the physical
plane, we must strip the metals of their outward properties in order to develop the essence within. As says
Helvetius : " . . the essences of metals are hidden in
their outward bodies, as the kernel is hidden in the
nut. Every earthly body, whether animal, vegetable,
or mineral, is the habitation and terrestrial abode of
that celestial spirit, or influence, which is its principle
of life or growth. The secret of Alchemy is the
destruction of the body, which enables the Artist
to get at, and utilise for his own purposes, the
living soul." [17] This killing of the outward nature
of material things was to be brought about by the
processes of putrefaction and decay ; hence the reason
why such processes figure so largely in alchemistic
recipes for the preparation of the "Divine Magistery."

---

[16] See BENEDICTUS FIGULUS : *A Golden and Blessed Casket of
Nature's Marvels* (translated by A. E. Waite, 1893, pp. 36, 37,
and 41).
[17] J. F. HELVETIUS : *The Golden Calf*, ch. iv. (see *The Hermetic
Museum*, vol. ii. p. 298).

PLATE 4.

A.

SYMBOLICAL ILLUSTRATION

Representing the
Coction of Gold Amalgam in a Closed Vessel.

B.

SYMBOLICAL ILLUSTRATION

Representing the
Transmutation of the Metals.

[To face page

It must be borne in mind, however, that the alchemists used the terms "putrefaction" and "decay" rather indiscriminately, applying them to chemical processes which are no longer regarded as such. Pictorial symbols of death and decay representative of such processes are to be found in several alchemistic books. There is a curious series of pictures in *A Form and Method of Perfecting Base Metals*, by Janus Lacinus, the Calabrian (a short tract prefixed to *The New Pearl of Great Price* by Peter Bonus — see § 39), of which we show three examples in plates 3 and 4. In the first picture of the series (not shown here) we enter the palace of the king (gold) and observe him sitting crowned upon his throne, surrounded by his son (mercury) and five servants (silver, copper, tin, iron and lead). In the next picture (plate 3, fig. B), the son, incited by the servants, kills his father ; and, in the third, he catches the blood of his murdered parent in his robes ; whereby we understand that an amalgam of gold and mercury is to be prepared, the gold apparently disappearing or dying, whilst the mercury is coloured thereby. The next picture shows us a grave being dug, *i.e.*, a furnace is to be made ready. In the fifth picture in the series, the son "thought to throw his father into the grave, and to leave him there ; but . . . both fell in together" ; and in the sixth picture (plate 4, fig. A), we see the son being prevented from escaping, both son and father being left in the grave to decay. Here we have instructions in symbolical form to place the amalgam in a sealed vessel in the furnace and to allow it to remain there until some change is observed. So the allegory proceeds. Ultimately the father is restored to life, the symbol of resurrection being (as might be expected) of frequent occurrence in alchemistic literature. By this resurrection we understand that the gold will finally be obtained in a pure form. Indeed, it is now the "great medicine" and, in the last picture of the series (plate 4, fig. B), the king's son and his five servants are all made kings in virtue of its powers.

§ **26.** The alchemists believed that a most minute proportion of the Stone projected upon considerable quantities of heated mercury, molten lead, or other "base" metal, would transmute practically the whole into silver or gold. This claim of the alchemists, that a most minute quantity of the Stone was sufficient to transmute considerable quantities of "base" metal, has been the object of much ridicule. Certainly, some of the claims of the alchemists (understood literally) are out of all reason; but on the other hand, the disproportion between the quantities of Stone and transmuted metal cannot be advanced as an *à priori* objection to the alchemists' claims, inasmuch that a class of chemical reactions (called "catalytic") is known, in which the presence of a small quantity of some appropriate form of matter—the catalyst—brings about a chemical change in an indefinite quantity of some other form or forms; thus, for example, cane-sugar in aqueous solution is converted into two other sugars by the action of small quantities of acid; and sulphur-dioxide and oxygen, which will not combine under ordinary conditions, do so readily in the presence of a small quantity

The Powers of the Philosopher's Stone.

of platinized asbestos, which is obtained unaltered after the reaction is completed and may be used over and over again (this process is actually employed in the manufacture of sulphuric acid or oil of vitriol). However, whether any such catalytic transmutation of the chemical "elements" is possible is merely conjecture.

§ **27.** The Elixir of Life, which was generally described as a solution of the Stone in spirits of

The Elixir of Life. wine, or identified with the Stone itself, could be applied, so it was thought, under certain conditions to the alchemist himself, with an entirely analogous result, *i.e.*, it would restore him to the flower of youth. The idea, not infrequently attributed to the alchemists, that the Elixir would endow one with a life of endless duration on the material plane is not in strict accord with alchemistic analogy. From this point of view, the effect of the Elixir is physiological perfection, which, although ensuring long life, is not equivalent to endless life on the material plane. "The Philosophers' Stone," says Paracelsus, "purges the whole body of man, and cleanses it from all impurities by the introduction of new and more youthful forces wh ch it joins to the nature of man." [18] And in an)ther work expressive of the opinions of the same alchemist, we read: " . . . there is nothing which might deliver the mortal body from death ; but there is One Thing which may postpone decay, renew youth, and prolong short human

---

[18] THEOPHRASTUS PARACELSUS: *The Fifth Book of the Archidoxies* (see *The Hermetic and Alchemical Writings of Paracelsus*, translated by A. E. Waite, 1894, vol. ii. p. 39).

life . . ." [19]   In the theory that a solution of the
Philosopher's Stone (which, it must be remembered,
was thought to be of a species with gold) constituted
the *Elixir Vitæ*, can be traced, perhaps, the idea that
gold in a potable form was a veritable cure-all : in
the latter days of Alchemy any yellow-coloured liquid
was foisted upon a credulous public as a medicinal
preparation of gold.

§ **28.** We will conclude this chapter with some
few remarks regarding the practical methods of

The Practical Methods of the Alchemists. the alchemists.   In their experiments,
the alchemists worked with very large
quantities of material compared with what
is employed in chemical researches at the
present day.   They had great belief in the efficacy
of time to effect a desired change in their substances,
and they were wont to repeat the same operation
(such as distillation, for example) on the same material over and over again ; which demonstrated their
unwearied patience, even if it effected little towards
the attainment of their end.   They paid much attention to any changes of colour they observed in their
experiments, and many descriptions of supposed
methods to achieve the *magnum opus* contain de-
tailed directions as to the various changes of colour
which must be obtained in the material operated upon
if a successful issue to the experiment is desired.[20]

---

[19] *The Book of the Revelation of Hermes, interpreted by Theophrastus Paracelsus, concerning the Supreme Secret of the World.*
(See BENEDICTUS FIGULUS : *A Golden Casket of Nature's Marvels*,
translated by A. E. Waite, 1893, pp. 33 and 34.)

[20] As writes Espagnet in his *Hermetic Arcanum*, canons 64 and 65 :
"The Means or demonstrative signs are Colours, successively and
orderly affecting the matter and its affections and demonstrative

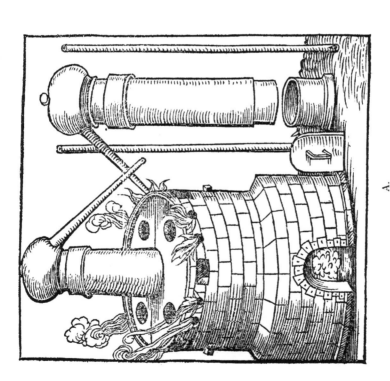

B.

A.

ALCHEMISTIC APPARATUS. A and B.—Two forms of Apparatus for Sublimation.

[To face page 37

In plates 5 and 6 we give illustrations of some characteristic pieces of apparatus employed by the alchemists.   Plate 5, fig. A, and plate 6, fig. A, are from a work known as *Alchemiae Gebri* (1545); plate 5, fig. B, is from Glauber's work on Furnaces (1651); and plate 6, fig. B, is from a work by Dr. John French entitled *The Art of Distillation* (1651).

passions, whereof there are also three special ones (as critical) to be noted; to these some add a Fourth.   The first is black, which is called the Crow's head, because of its extreme blackness, whose crepusculum sheweth the beginning of the action of the fire of nature and solution, and the blackest midnight sheweth the perfection of liquefaction, and confusion of the elements.   Then the grain putrefies and is corrupted, that it may be the more apt for generation.   The white colour succeedeth the black, wherein is given the perfection of the first degree, and of the White Sulphur.   This is called the blessed stone; this Earth is white and foliated, wherein Philosophers do sow their gold.   The third is Orange colour, which is produced in the passage of the white to the red, as the middle, and being mixed of both is as the dawn with his saffron hair, a forerunner of the Sun.   The fourth colour is Ruddy and Sanguine, which is extracted from the white fire only.   Now because whiteness is easily altered by any other colour before day it quickly faileth of its candour.   But the deep redness of the Sun perfecteth the work of Sulphur, which is called the Sperm of the male, the fire of the Stone, the King's Crown, and the Son of Sol, wherein the first labour of the workman resteth.

"Besides these decretory signs which firmly inhere in the matter, and shew its essential mutations, almost infinite colours appear, and shew themselves in vapours, as the Rainbow in the clouds, which quickly pass away and are expelled by those that succeed, more affecting the air than the earth: the operator must have a gentle care of them, because they are not permanent, and proceed not from the intrinsic disposition of the matter, but from the fire painting and fashioning everything after its pleasure, or casually by heat in slight moisture" (see *Collectanea Hermetica*, edited by W. Wynn Westcott, vol. i., 1893, pp. 28 and 29).   Very probably this is not without a mystical meaning as well as a supposed application in the preparation of the physical Stone.

The first figure shows us a furnace and alembics. The alembic proper is a sort of still-head which can be luted on to a flask or other vessel, and was much used for distillations. In the present case, however, the alembics are employed in conjunction with apparatus for subliming difficultly volatile substances. Plate 5, fig. B, shows another apparatus for sublimation, consisting of a sort of oven, and four detachable upper chambers, generally called aludels. In both forms of apparatus the vapours are cooled in the upper part of the vessel, and the substance is deposited in the solid form, being thereby purified from less volatile impurities. Plate 6, fig. A, shows an athanor (or digesting furnace) and a couple of digesting vessels. A vessel of this sort was employed for heating bodies in a closed space, the top being sealed up when the substances to be operated upon had been put inside, and the vessel heated in an athanor in ashes, a uniform temperature being maintained. The pelican, illustrated in plate 6, fig. B, was used for a similar purpose, the two arms being added in the idea that the vapours would be circulated thereby.

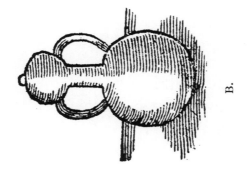

B.

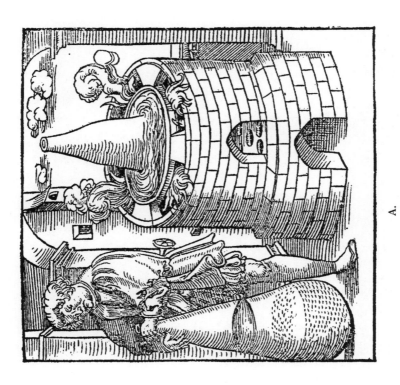

A.

ALCHEMISTIC APPARATUS.   A.—Athanors.   B.—A Pelican.

CHAPTER III

THE ALCHEMISTS[1]

(A. BEFORE PARACELSUS)

§ **29.** Having now considered the chief points in the theory of Physical Alchemy, we must turn our attention to the lives and individual teachings of the alchemists themselves. The first name which is found in the history of Alchemy is that of **Hermes Trismegistos.** We have already mentioned the high esteem in which the works ascribed to this personage

Hermes Trismegistos.

[1] It is perhaps advisable to mention here that the lives of the alchemists, for the most part, are enveloped in considerable obscurity, and many points in connection therewith are in dispute. The authorities we have followed will be found, as a rule, specifically mentioned in what follows ; but we may here acknowledge our general indebtedness to the following works, though, as the reader will observe, many others have been consulted as well : Thomas Thomson's *The History of Chemistry*, Meyer's *A History of Chemistry*, the anonymous *Lives of Alchemystical Philosophers* (1815), the works of Mr. A. E. Waite, the *Dictionary of National Biography*, and certain articles in the *Encyclopædia Britannica*. This must not be taken to mean, however, that we have always followed the conclusions reached in these works, for so far as the older of them are concerned, recent researches by various authorities—to whom reference will be found in the following pages, and to whom, also, we are indebted—have shown, in certain cases, that such are not tenable.

were held by the alchemists (§ 6). He has been regarded as the father of Alchemy; his name has supplied a synonym for the Art—the Hermetic Art —and even to-day we speak of *hermetically* sealing flasks and the like. But who Hermes actually was, or even if there were such a personage, is a matter of conjecture. The alchemists themselves supposed him to have been an Egyptian living about the time of Moses. He is now generally regarded as purely mythical—a personification of Thoth, the Egyptian God of learning; but, of course, some person or persons must have written the works attributed to him, and the first of such writers (if, as seems not unlikely, there were more than one) may be considered to have a right to the name. Of these works, the *Divine Pymander*,[2] a mystical-religious treatise, is the most important. The *Golden Tractate*, also attributed to Hermes, which is an exceedingly obscure alchemistic work, is now regarded as having been written at a comparatively late date.

§ **30.** In a work attributed to Albertus Magnus, but which is probably spurious, we are told that Alexander the Great found the tomb of Hermes in a cave near Hebron. This tomb contained an emerald table— "The Smaragdine Table"—on which were inscribed the following thirteen sentences in Phœnician characters :—

The Smaragdine Table.

1. I speak not fictitious things, but what is true and most certain.

---

[2] Dr. Everard's translation of this work forms vol. ii. of the *Collectanea Hermetica*, edited by W. Wynn Westcott, M.B., D.P.H. It is now, however, out of print.

2. What is below is like that which is above, and what is above is like that which is below, to accomplish the miracles of one thing.

3. And as all things were produced by the mediation of one Being, so all things were produced from this one thing by adaptation.

4. Its father is the Sun, its mother the Moon ; the wind carries it in its belly, its nurse is the earth.

5. It is the cause of all perfection throughout the whole world.

6. Its power is perfect if it be changed into earth.

7. Separate the earth from the fire, the subtle from the gross, acting prudently and with judgment.

8. Ascend with the greatest sagacity from the earth to heaven, and then again descend to the earth, and unite together the powers of things superior and things inferior.   Thus you will obtain the glory of the whole world, and all obscurity will fly far away from you.

9. This thing is the fortitude of all fortitude, because it overcomes all subtle things, and penetrates every solid thing.

10. Thus were all things created.

11. Thence proceed wonderful adaptations which are produced in this way.

12. Therefore am I called Hermes Trismegistus, possessing the three parts of the philosophy of the whole world.

13. That which I had to say concerning the operation of the Sun is completed.

These sentences clearly teach the doctrine of the alchemistic essence or "One Thing," which is everywhere present, penetrating even solids (this we should note is true of the ether of space), and out of which all things of the physical world are made by adaptation or modification. The terms Sun and Moon in the above passage probably stand for Spirit and Matter respectively, not gold and silver.

§ **31.** One of the earliest of the alchemists of whom record remains was **Zosimus of Panopolis,** who flourished in the fifth century, and was regarded by the later alchemists as a master of the Art. He is said to have written many treatises dealing with Alchemy, but only fragments remain. Of these fragments, Professor Venable says: " . . . they give us a good idea of the learning of the man and of his times. They contain descriptions of apparatus, of furnaces, studies of minerals, of alloys, of glass making, of mineral waters, and much that is mystical, besides a good deal referring to the transmutation of metals." [3] Zosimus is said to have been the author of the saying, "like begets like," but whether all the fragments ascribed to him were really his work is doubtful.

Zosimus of Panopolis.

Among other early alchemists we may mention also **Africanus,** the Syrian; **Synesius,** Bishop of Ptolemais, and the historian, **Olympiodorus** of Thebes.

§ **32.** In the seventh century the Arabians conquered Egypt; and strangely enough, Alchemy flourished under them to a remarkable degree. Of all the Arabian alchemists, **Geber** has been regarded as the greatest; as Professor Meyer says: "There can be no dispute that with the name *Geber* was propagated the memory of a personality

Geber.

[3] F. P. VENABLE, Ph.D.: *A Short History of Chemistry* (1896), p. 13.

with which the chemical knowledge of the time was bound up." [4]   Geber is supposed to have lived about the ninth century, but of his life nothing definite is known.   A large number of works have been ascribed to him, of which the majority are unknown, but the four Latin MSS. which have been printed under the titles *Summa Perfectionis Mettalorum, De Investigatione Perfectionis Metallorum, De Inventione Veritatis* and *De Fornacibus Construendis*, were, until a few years ago, regarded as genuine.   On the strength of these works, Geber has ranked high as a chemist.   In them are described the preparation of many important chemical compounds; the most essential chemical operations, such as sublimation, distillation, filtration, crystallisation (or coagulation, as the alchemists called it), &c.; and also important chemical apparatus, for example, the water-bath, improved furnaces, &c.   However, it was shown by the late Professor Berthelot that *Summa Perfectionis Mettalorum* is a forgery of the fourteenth century, and the other works forgeries of an even later date. Moreover, the original Arabic MSS. of Geber have been brought to light.   These true writings of Geber are very obscure ; they give no warrant for believing that the famous sulphur-mercury theory was due to this alchemist, and they prove him not to be the expert chemist that he was supposed to have been. The spurious writings mentioned above show that the pseudo-Geber was a man of wide chemical knowledge and experience, and play a not inconsiderable part in the history of Alchemy.

[4] Ernst von Meyer: *A History of Chemistry* (translated by Dr. McGowan, 1906), p. 31.

§ **33.** Among other Arabian alchemists the most celebrated were **Avicenna** and **Rhasis,** who are supposed to have lived some time after Geber; and to whom, perhaps, the sulphur-mercury theory may have been to some extent due.

Other Arabian Alchemists

The teachings of the Arabian alchemists gradually penetrated into the Western world, in which, during the thirteenth century, flourished some of the most eminent of the alchemists, whose lives and teachings we must now briefly consider.

§ **34. Albertus Magnus,** Albert Groot or Albert von Bollstadt (see plate 7), was born at Lauingen, probably in 1193. He was educated at Padua, and in his later years he showed himself apt at acquiring the knowledge of his time. He studied theology, philosophy and natural science, and is chiefly celebrated as an Aristotelean philosopher. He entered the Dominican order, taught publicly at Cologne, Paris and elsewhere, and was made provincial of this order. Later he had the bishopric of Regensburg conferred on him, but he retired after a few years to a Dominican cloister, where he devoted himself to philosophy and science. He was one of the most learned men of his time and, moreover, a man of noble character. The authenticity of the alchemistic works attributed to him has been questioned.

Albertus Magnus (1193–1280)

§ **35.** The celebrated Dominican, **Thomas Aquinas** (see plate 8), was probably a pupil of Albertus Magnus, from whom it is thought he imbibed alchemistic learning. It is very probable, however, that the alchemistic works attributed to him are spurious. The

Thomas Aquinas (1225–1274).

PLATE 7.

MAGNVS · ALBERTVS BOLSTADIVS COGNOMENTO

Mitra pedumq; oneri tibi quondam, Alberte, fuerunt.
Dulcius est Sophiæ delituiſse ſinu.

[by de Bry]

PORTRAIT OF
ALBERTUS MAGNUS.

author of these works manifests a deeply religious tone, and, according to Thomson's *History of Chemistry*, he was the first to employ the term "amalgam" to designate an alloy of mercury with some other metal.[5]

§ **36. Roger Bacon,** the most illustrious of the mediæval alchemists, was born near Ilchester in Somerset, probably in 1214. His erudition, considering the general state of ignorance prevailing at this time, was most remarkable. Professor Meyer says : " He is to be regarded as the intellectual originator of experimental research, if the departure in this direction is to be coupled with any one name—a direction which, followed more and more as time went on, gave to the science [of Chemistry] its own peculiar stamp, and ensured its steady development."[6] Roger Bacon studied theology and science at Oxford and at Paris ; and he joined the Franciscan order, at what date, however, is uncertain. He was particularly interested in optics, and certain discoveries in this branch of physics have been attributed to him, though probably erroneously. It appears, also, that he was acquainted with gunpowder, which was, however, not employed in Europe until many years later.[7] Unfortunately, he earned the undesirable reputation of being in communication with the powers of darkness, and as he did not hesitate to oppose many of the opinions current at the time, he

r---- ----n
(1214–1294)

[5] THOMAS THOMSON : *The History of Chemistry*, vol. i. (1830), p. 33.
[6] ERNST VON MEYER: *A History of Chemistry* (translated by Lr. McGowan, 1906), p. 35.
[7] See ROGER BACON's *Discovery of Miracles*, chaps. vi. and xi.

suffered much persecution.   He was a firm believer in
the powers of the Philosopher's Stone to transmute
large quantities of " base " metal into gold, and also to
extend the life of the individual.   " *Alchimy*, ' he says,
" is a Science, teaching how to transforme any kind of
mettall into another : and that by a proper medicine, as
it appeareth by many Philosophers Bookes.   *Alchimy*
therefore is a science teaching how to make and compound a certaine medicine, which is called *Elixir*, the
which when it is cast upon mettals or imperfect bodies,
doth fully perfect them in the verie projection." [8]   He
also believed in Astrology ; but, nevertheless, he was
entirely opposed to many of the magical and superstitious notions held at the time, and his tract, *De
Secretis Operibus Artis et Naturæ, et de Nullitate
Magiæ*, was an endeavour to prove that many so-called
" miracles " could be brought about simply by the aid
of natural science.   Roger Bacon was a firm supporter
of the Sulphur-Mercury theory : he says : " . . . the
natural principles in the mynes, are *Argent-vive*, and
Sulphur.   All mettals and minerals, whereof there be
sundrie and divers kinds, are begotten of these two :
but I must tel you, that nature alwaies intendeth and
striveth to the perfection of Gold : but many accidents
coming between, change the metalls. . . .   For according to the puritie and impuritie of the two aforesaide
principles, *Argent-vive* and *Sulphur*, pure, and impure
mettals are ingendred." [9]   He expresses surprise that
any should employ animal and vegetable substances
in their attempts to prepare the Stone, a practice
common to some alchemists but warmly criticised by

[8] ROGER BACON : *The Mirror of Alchimy* (1597), p. 1.
[9] *Ibid.* p. 2.

others. He says : "Nothing may be mingled with
mettalls which hath not beene made or sprung from
them, it remaineth cleane inough, that no strange
thing which hath not his originall from these two [viz.,
sulphur and mercury], is able to perfect them, or to
make a chaunge and new transmutation of them : so
that it is to be wondered at, that any wise man should
set his mind upon living creatures, or vegetables which
are far off, when there be minerals to bee found nigh
enough : neither may we in any wise thinke, that any
of the Philosophers placed the Art in the said remote
things, except it were by way of comparison." [10]   The
one process necessary for the preparation of the
Stone, he tells us, is "continuall concoction" in the
fire, which is the method that "God hath given to
nature." [11]   He died about 1294.

§ **37.** The date and birthplace of **Arnold de
Villanova,** or Villeneuve, are both uncertain. He
studied medicine at Paris, and in the latter
part of the thirteenth century practised
professionally in Barcelona. To avoid
persecution at the hands of the Inquisition, he was obliged to leave Spain, and ultimately
found safety with Frederick II. in Sicily. He was
famous not only as an alchemist, but also as a skilful
physician. He died (it is thought in a shipwreck)
about 1310–1313.

*Arnold de
V'llanova.
(12—?–1310?).*

§ **38. Raymond Lully,** the son of a noble Spanish
family, was born at Palma (in Majorca) about 1235.
He was a man of somewhat eccentric character—
in his youth a man of pleasure ; in his maturity,

[10] Roger Bacon : *The Mirror of Alchimy* (1597), p. 4.
[11] *Ibid.* p. 9.

a mystic and ascetic. His career was of a roving and adventurous character. We are told that, in his younger days, although married, he be-

R ymond
I.ully
(1235 ?–1315).

came violently infatuated with a lady of the name of Ambrosia de Castello, who vainly tried to dissuade him from his profane passion. Her efforts proving futile, she requested Lully to call upon her, and in the presence of her husband, bared to his sight her breast, which was almost eaten away by a cancer. This sight—so the story goes—brought about Lully's conversion. He became actuated by the idea of converting to Christianity the heathen in Africa, and engaged the services of an Arabian whereby he might learn the language. The man, however, discovering his master's object, attempted to assassinate him, and Lully narrowly escaped with his life. But his enthusiasm for missionary work never abated—his central idea was the reasonableness and demonstrability of Christian doctrine — and unhappily he was, at last, stoned to death by the inhabitants of Bugiah (in Algeria) in 1315.[12]

A very large number of alchemistic, theological and other treatises are attributed to Lully, many of which are undoubtedly spurious ; and it is a difficult question to decide exactly which are genuine. He is supposed to have derived a knowledge of Alchemy from Roger Bacon and Arnold de Villanova. It appears more probable, however, either that Lully the alchemist was a personage distinct from the Lully whose life we have sketched above, or that the alchemistic writings attributed to him are forgeries of a similar nature to

[12] See *Lives of Alchemystical Philosophers* (1815), pp. 17 *et seq.*

the works of pseudo - Geber (§ 32). Of these alchemical writings we may here mention the *Clavicula*. This he says is the key to all his other books on Alchemy, in which books the whole Art is fully declared, though so obscurely as not to be understandable without its aid. In this work an alleged method for what may be called the multiplication of the " noble " metals rather than transmutation is described in clear language; but it should be noticed that the stone employed is itself a compound either of silver or gold. According to Lully, the secret of the Philosopher's Stone is the extraction of the mercury of silver or gold. He writes: " Metals cannot be transmuted. . . . in the Minerals, unless they be reduced into their first Matter. . . . Therefore I counsel you, O my Friends, that you do not work but about *Sol* and *Luna*, reducing them into the first Matter, our *Sulphur* and *Argent vive*: therefore, Son, you are to use this venerable Matter; and I swear unto you and promise, that unless you take the *Argent vive* of these two, you go to the Practick as blind men without eyes or sense. . . . " [13]

§ **39.** In 1546, a work was published entitled *Magarita Pretiosa*, which claimed to be a "faithful abridgement," by "Janus Lacinus
Peter Bonus (14th Century). Therapus, the Calabrian," of a MS. written by **Peter Bonus** in the fourteenth century. An abridged English translation of this book by Mr. A. E. Waite was published in 1894. Of the life of Bonus, who is said to have been an inhabitant of Pola, a seaport

[13] RAYMOND LULLY: *Clavicula, or, A Little Key* (see *Aurifontina Chymica*, 1680, p. 167).

of Istria, nothing is known ; but the *Magarita Pretiosa* is an alchemistic work of considerable interest.   The author commences, like pseudo-Geber in his *Sum of Perfection*, by bringing forward a number of very ingenious arguments against the validity of the Art; he then proceeds with arguments in favour of Alchemy and puts forward answers in full to the former objections ; further difficulties, &c., are then dealt with.   In all this, compared with many other alchemists, Bonus, though somewhat prolix, is remarkably lucid.   All metals, he argues, following the views of pseudo-Geber, consist of mercury and sulphur ; but whilst the mercury is always one and the same, different metals contain different sulphurs.   There are also two different kinds of sulphurs—inward and outward.   Sulphur is necessary for the development of the mercury, but for the final product, gold, to come forth, it is necessary that the outward and impure sulphur be purged off.   " Each metal," says Bonus, " differs from all the rest, and has a certain perfection and completeness of its own ; but none, except gold, has reached that highest degree of perfection of which it is capable.   For all common metals there is a transient and a perfect state of inward completeness, and this perfect state they attain either through the slow operation of Nature, or through the sudden transformatory power of our Stone. We must, however, add that the imperfect metals form part of the great plan and design of Nature, though they are in course of transformation into gold. For a large number of very useful and indispensable tools and utensils could not be provided at all if there were no copper, iron, tin, or lead, and if all metals were either silver or gold.   For this beneficent reason Nature has furnished us with the metallic substance in all its different stages of development, from iron, or the lowest, to gold, or the highest state of metallic perfection.   Nature is ever studying variety, and, for that reason, instead of covering the whole face of the earth with water, has evolved out of that elementary substance a great diversity of forms, embracing the whole animal, vegetable and mineral world.   It is, in like manner, for the use of men that Nature has differentiated the metallic substance into a great variety of species and forms." [14]   According to this interesting alchemistic work, the Art of Alchemy consists, not in reducing the imperfect metals to their first substance, but in carrying forward Nature's work, developing the imperfect metals to perfection and removing their impure sulphur.

§ **40. Nicolas Flamel** (see plate 8) was born about 1330, probably in Paris.   His parents were poor, and

Nicolas took up the trade of a scrivener.
Nicolas Flamel (1330–1418).
In the course of time, Flamel became a very wealthy man and, at the same time, it appears, one who exhibited consider-
able munificence.   This increase in Flamel's wealth has been attributed to supposed success in the Hermetic Art.   We are told that a remarkable book came into the young scriveners possession, which, at first, he was unable to understand, until, at last, he had the good fortune to meet an adept who translated its mysteries for him.   This book revealed the occult secrets of Alchemy, and by its means Nicolas was enabled

[14] PETER BONUS : *The New Pearl of Great Price* (Mr. A. E. Waite's translation, pp. 176–177).

to obtain immense quantities of gold. This story, however, appears to be of a legendary nature, and it seems more likely that Flamel's riches resulted from his business as a scrivener and from moneylending. At any rate, all of the alchemistic works attributed to Flamel are of more or less questionable origin. One of these, entitled *A Short Tract, or Philosophical Summary*, will be found in *The Hermetic Museum*. It is a very brief work, supporting the sulphur-mercury theory.

§ **41.** Probably the most celebrated of all alchemistic books is the work known as *Triumph-Wagen des Antimonii.* A Latin translation with a commentary by Theodore Kerckringius was published in 1685, and an English translation of this version by Mr. A. E. Waite appeared in 1893. The author describes himself as " **Basil Valentine,** a Benedictine monk." In his "*Practica*," another alchemistic work, he says : " When I had emptied to the dregs the cup of human suffering, I was led to consider the wretchedness of this world, and the fearful consequences of our first parents' disobedience . . . I made haste to withdraw myself from the evil world, to bid farewell to it, and to devote myself to the Service of God."[15] He proceeds to relate that he entered a monastery, but finding that he had some time on his hands after performing his daily work and devotions, and not wishing to pass this time in idleness, he took up the study of Alchemy, "the investigation of those natural secrets by which God has

Marginal note: " Basil Valentine " and " The Triumphal Chariot of Antimony."

---

[15] " BASIL VALENTINE ": *The " Practica "* (see *The Hermetic Museum*, vol. i. p. 313).

PLATE 8.

PORTRAIT OF NICOLAS FLAMEL.

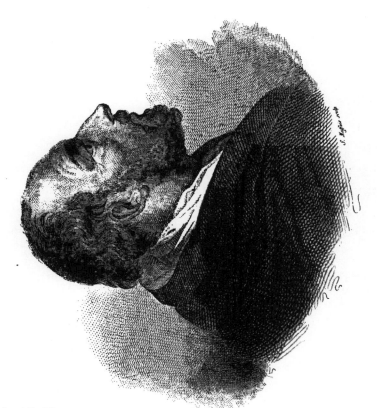

PORTRAIT OF THOMAS AQUINAS.

shadowed out eternal things," and at last his labours were rewarded by the discovery of a Stone most potent in the curing of diseases. In *The Triumphal Chariot of Antimony* are accurately described a large number of antimonial preparations, and as Basil was supposed to have written this work some time in the fifteenth century, these preparations were accordingly concluded to have been, for the most part, his own discoveries. He defends with the utmost vigour the medicinal values of antimony, and criticises in terms far from mild the physicians of his day. On account of this work Basil Valentine has ranked very high as an experimental chemist ; but from quite early times its date and authorship have been regarded alike as doubtful ; and it appears from the researches of the late Professor Schorlemmer "to be an undoubted forgery dating from about 1600, the information being culled from the works of other writers. . . ."[16] Probably the other works ascribed to Basil Valentine are of a like nature. *The Triumphal Chariot of Antimony* does, however, give an accurate account of the knowledge of antimony of this time, and the pseudo-Valentine shows himself to have been a man of considerable experience with regard to this subject.

§ **42. Isaac of Holland** and a countryman of the same name, probably his son, are said to have been the first Dutch alchemists. They are supposed to have lived during the fifteenth century, but of their lives nothing is known. Isaac, although not free from superstitious opinions, appears to have been a practical

Isaac of Holland (15th Century).

[16] Sir H. E. ROSCOE, F.R.S., and C. SCHORLEMMER, F.R.S.: *A Treatise on Chemistry*, vol. i. (1905), p. 9.

chemist, and his works, which abound in recipes, were held in great esteem by Paracelsus and other alchemists. He held that all things in this world are of a dual nature, partly good and partly bad. " . . . All that God hath created good in the upper part of the world," he writes, " are perfect and uncorruptible, as the heaven: but whatsoever in these lower parts, whether it be in beasts, fishes, and all manner of sensible creatures, hearbs or plants, it is indued with a double nature, that is to say, perfect, and unperfect; the perfect nature is called the Quintessence, the unperfect the Feces or dreggs, or the venemous or combustible oile. . . . God hath put a secret nature or influence in every creature, and . . . to every nature of one sort or kind he hath given one common influence and vertue, whether it bee on Physick or other secret works, which partly are found out by naturall workmanship. And yet more things are unknown than are apparent to our senses."[17] He gives directions for extracting the Quintessence, for which marvellous powers are claimed, out of sugar and other organic substances; and he appears to be the earliest known writer who makes mention of the famous sulphur-mercury-salt theory.

§ **43. Bernard Trevisan,** a French count of the fifteenth century, squandered enormous sums of money in the search for the Stone, in which the whole of his life and energies were engaged. He seems to have become the dupe of one charlatan after another,

---

[17] *One hundred and Fourteen Experiments and Cures of the Famous Physitian Theophrastus Paracelsus, whereunto is added . . . certain Secrets of Isaac Hollandus, concerning the Vegetall and Animall Work* (1652), p. 35.

but at last, at a ripe old age, he says that his labours were rewarded, and that he successfully performed the *magnum opus*. In a short, but rather

Bernard

(1406–1490).

obscure work, he speaks of the Philosopher s Stone in the following words : " This Stone then is compounded of a Body and Spirit, or of a volatile and fixed Substance, and that is therefore done, because nothing in the World can be generated and brought to light without these two Substances, to wit, a Male and Female : From whence it appeareth, that although these two Substances are not of one and the same species, yet one Stone doth thence arise, and although they appear and are said to be two Substances, yet in truth it is but one, to wit, *Argent-vive*." [18]   He appears, however, to have added nothing to our knowledge of chemical science.

§ **44. Sir George Ripley,** an eminent alchemistic philosopher of the fifteenth century, entered upon a monastic life when a youth, becom-

Sir George

'14 ?–1490?).

ing one of the canons regular of Bridlington. After some travels he returned to England and obtaining leave from the Pope to live in solitude, he devoted himself to the study of the Hermetic Art. His chief work is *The Compound of Alchymie . . . conteining twelve Gates*, which was written in 1471. In this curious work, we learn that there are twelve processes necessary for the achievement of the *magnum opus*, namely, Calcination, Solution, Separation, Conjunction, Putrefaction, Congelation, Cibation, Sublimation, Fermen-

---

[18] BERNARD, EARL OF TREVISAN : *A Treatise of the Philosophers Stone*, 1683 (see *Collectanea Chymica : A Collection of Ten Several Treatises in Chemistry*, 1684, p. 91).

tation, Exaltation, Multiplication, and Projection.
These are likened to the twelve gates of a castle
which the philosopher must enter.   At the conclusion
of the twelfth gate, Ripley says :—

> " Now thou hast conqueryd the *twelve Gates*,
> And all the Castell thou holdyst at wyll,
> Keep thy Secretts in store unto thy selve ;
> And the commaundements of God looke thou fulfull :
> In fyer conteinue thy glas styll,
>> And Multeply thy Medcyns ay more and more,
>> For wyse men done say *store ys no sore.*" [19]

At the conclusion of the work he tells us that in all
that he wrote before he was mistaken ; he says :—

> " I made *Solucyons* full many a one,
> Of Spyrytts, Ferments, Salts, Yerne and Steele ;
> Wenyng so to make the Phylosophers Stone :
> But fynally I lost eche dele,
> After my Boks yet wrought I well ;
>> Whych evermore untrue I provyd,
>> That made me oft full sore agrevyd." [20]

Ripley did much to popularise the works of Raymond Lully in England, but does not appear to have
added to the knowledge of practical chemistry.   His
Bosom Book, which contains an alleged method for
preparing the Stone, will be found in the *Collectanea
Chemica* (1893).

§ **45**. **Thomas Norton,** the author of the celebrated
Ordinall of Alchemy, was probably born shortly before

---

[19] Sir GEORGE RIPLEY : *The Compound of Alchemy* (see
Theatrum Chemicum Britannicum, edited by Elias Ashmole, 1652,
p. 186).
[20] *Ibid.* p. 189.

the commencement of the fifteenth century. The *Ordinall*, which is written in verse (and which will

Thomas
Norton 15th
Century).

be found in Ashmole's *Theatrum Chemicum Britannicum*), [21] was published anonymously, but the author's identity is revealed by a curious device. The initial syllables of the proem and of the first six chapters, together with the first line of the seventh chapter, give the following couplet :—

> "Tomais Norton of Briseto,
> A parfet *Master* ye maie him call trowe."

Samuel Norton, the grandson of Thomas, who was also an alchemist, says that Thomas Norton was a member of the privy chamber of Edward IV. Norton's distinctive views regarding the generation of the metals we have already mentioned (see § 20). He taught that true knowledge of the Art of Alchemy could only be obtained by word of mouth from an adept, and in his *Ordinall* he gives an account of his own initiation. He tells us that he was instructed by his master (probably Sir George Ripley) and learnt the secrets of the Art in forty days, at the age of twenty-eight. He does not, however, appear to have reaped the fruits of this knowledge. Twice, he tells us, did he prepare the Elixir, and twice was it stolen from him ; and he is said to have died in 1477, after ruining himself and his friends by his unsuccessful experiments.

[21] A prose version will be found in *The Hermetic Museum*, translated back into English from a Latin translation by Maier.

CHAPTER IV

THE ALCHEMISTS (*continued*)

(B. PARACELSUS AND AFTER)

§ **46.** That erratic genius, **Paracelsus**—or, to give him his correct name, Philip (?) Aureole (?) **Theophrast Bombast von Hohenheim**— whose portrait forms the frontispiece to the present work—was born at Einsiedeln in Switzerland in 1493. He studied the alchemistic and medical arts under his father, who was a physician, and continued his studies later at the University of Basle. He also gave some time to the study of magic and the occult sciences under the famous Trithemius of Spanheim. Paracelsus, however, found the merely theoretical " book learning " of the university curriculum unsatisfactory and betook himself to the mines, where he might study the nature of metals at first hand. He then spent several years in travelling, visiting some of the chief countries of Europe. At last he returned to Basle, the chair of Medical Science of his old university being bestowed upon him. The works of Isaac of Holland had inspired him with the desire to improve upon the medical science of his day, and in his lectures (which were, contrary to the usual custom, delivered not in Latin, but in the German language) he denounced in violent terms the teachings of Galen and Avicenna, who were until then the accredited authorities on medical matters. His use of the German tongue, his coarseness in criticism and his intense self-esteem, combined with the fact that he did lay bare many of the medical follies and frauds of his day, brought him into very general dislike with the rest of the physicians, and the municipal authorities siding with the aggrieved apothecaries and physicians, whose methods Paracelsus had exposed, he fled from Basle and resumed his former roving life. He was, so we are told, a man of very intemperate habits, being seldom sober (a statement seriously open to doubt); but on the other hand, he certainly accomplished a very large number of most remarkable cures, and, judging from his writings, he was inspired by lofty and noble ideals and a fervent belief in the Christian religion. He died in 1541.

Paracelsus combined in himself such opposite characteristics that it is a matter of difficulty to criticise him aright. As says Professor Ferguson : " It is most difficult . . . to ascertain what his true character really was, to appreciate aright this man of fervid imagination, of powerful and persistent conviction, of unbated honesty and love of truth, of keen insight into the errors (as he thought them) of his time, of a merciless will to lay bare these errors and to reform the abuses to which they gave rise, who in an instant offends by his boasting, his grossness, his want of self-respect. It is a problem how to reconcile his ignorance, his weakness, his superstition, his crude notions, his erroneous observations, his ridiculous inferences and theories, with his grasp of method, his lofty views of the true scope of medicine, his lucid statements, his incisive and epigrammatic criticisms of men and motives." [1] It is also a problem of considerable difficulty to determine which of the many books attributed to him are really his genuine works, and consequently what his views on certain points exactly were.

§ **47**. Paracelsus was the first to recognise the desirability of investigating the physical universe with a motive other than alchemistic. He taught that "the object of chemistry is not to make gold, but to prepare medicines," and founded the school of Iatro-chemistry or Medical Chemistry. This synthesis of chemistry with medicine was of very great benefit to each science; new possibilities of chemical investigation were opened up now that the aim was not purely alchemistic. Paracelsus's central theory was that of the analogy between man, the microcosm, and the world or macrocosm. He regarded all the actions that go on in the human body as of a chemical nature, and he thought that illness was the result of a disproportion in the body between the quantities of the three great principles—sulphur, mercury, and salt— which he regarded as constituting all things; for example, he considered an excess of sulphur as the cause of fever, since sulphur was the fiery principle, &c. The basis of the iatro-chemical doctrines, namely, that the healthy human body is a particular combination of

Paracelsus

[1] JOHN FERGUSON, M.A.: Article "Paracelsus," *Encyclopædia Britannica*, 9th edition (1885), vol. xviii. p. 236.

chemical substances : illness the result of some change in this combination, and hence curable only by chemical medicines, expresses a certain truth, and is undoubtedly a great improvement upon the ideas of the ancients. But in the elaboration of his medical doctrines Paracelsus fell a prey to exaggeration and the fantastic, and many of his theories appear to be highly ridiculous. This extravagance is also very pronounced in the alchemistic works attributed to him ; for example, the belief in the artificial creation of minute living creatures resembling men (called " homunculi ")—a belief of the utmost absurdity, if we are to understand it literally. On the other hand, his writings do contain much true teaching of a mystical nature ; his doctrine of the correspondence of man with the universe considered as a whole, for example, certainly being radically true, though fantastically stated and developed by Paracelsus himself.

§ **48**. Between the pupils of Paracelsus and the older school of medicine, as might well be supposed, a battle royal was waged for a considerable time which ultimately concluded, if not with a full vindication of Paracelsus s teaching, yet with the acceptance of the fundamental iatro-chemical doctrines. Henceforward it is necessary to distinguish between the chemists and the alchemists —to distinguish those who pursued chemical studies with the object of discovering and preparing useful medicines, and later those who pursued such studies for their own sake, from those whose object was the transmutation of the " base " metals into gold, whether from purely selfish motives, or with the desire to

Iatro-
Chemistry.

demonstrate on the physical plane the validity of the
doctrines of Mysticism.   However, during the following century or two we find, very often, the chemist
and the alchemist united in one and the same person.
Men such as Glauber and Boyle, whose names will
ever be remembered by chemists, did not doubt the
possibility of performing the *magnum opus*.   In the
present chapter, however, we shall confine our attention for the most part to those men who may be
regarded, for one reason or another, particularly as
alchemists.   And the alchemists of the period we are
now considering present a very great diversity.   On
the one hand, we have men of much chemical knowledge and skill such as Libavius and van Helmont, on
the other hand we have those who stand equally as
high as exponents of mystic wisdom—men such as
Jacob Boehme and, to a less extent, Thomas Vaughan.
We have those, who, although they did not enrich the
science of Chemistry with any new discoveries, were,
nevertheless, regarded as masters of the Hermetic
Art ; and, finally, we have alchemists of the Edward
Kelley and George Starkey type, whose main object
was their own enrichment at their neighbours' expense.
Before, however, proceeding to an account of the lives
and teachings of these men, there is one curious matter
—perhaps the most remarkable of all historical curi-
osities—that calls for some brief consideration.   We
refer to the "far-famed" Rosicrucian Society.

§ **49**. The   exoteric   history   of   the   Rosicrucian
Society   commences   with   the   year   1614.   In   that
year   there   was   published   at   Cassel   in   Germany
a   pamphlet   entitled   *The   Discovery   of   the   Fraternity
of the Meritorious Order of the Rosy Cross, addressed to*

the Learned in General and the Governors of Europe.
After a discussion of the momentous question of the
general reformation of the world, which
was to be accomplished through the
medium of a secret confederacy of the
wisest and most philanthropic men, the
pamphlet proceeds to inform its readers that such
an association is in existence, founded over one
hundred years ago by the famous C.R.C., grand
initiate in the mysteries of Alchemy, whose history
(which is clearly of a fabulous or symbolical nature) is
given.   The book concludes by inviting the wise men
of the time to join the Fraternity, directing those who
wished to do so to indicate their desire by the publication of printed letters, which should come into the
hands of the Brotherhood. As might well be expected,
the pamphlet was the cause of considerable interest and
excitement, but although many letters were printed,
apparently none of them were vouchsafed a reply.
The following year a further pamphlet appeared, *The
Confession of the Rosicrucian Fraternity, addressed to
the Learned in Europe*, and in 1616, *The Chymical
Nuptials of Christian Rosencreutz.* This latter book
is a remarkable allegorical romance, describing how an
old man, a lifelong student of the alchemistic Art, was
present at the accomplishment of the *magnum opus* in
the year 1459. An enormous amount of controversy took place; it was plain to some that the
Society had deluded them, whilst others hotly maintained its claims ; but after about four years had passed,
the excitement had subsided, and the subject ceased,
for the time being, to arouse any particular interest.

Some writers, even in recent times, more gifted for

The
Rosicrucian
Society.

romance than for historical research, have seen in the Rosicrucian Society a secret confederacy of immense antiquity and of stupendous powers, consisting of the great initiates of all ages, supposed to be in possession of the arch secrets of alchemistic art. It is abundantly evident, however, that it was nothing of the sort. It is clear from an examination of the pamphlets already mentioned that they are animated by Lutheran ideals ; and it is of interest to note that Luther's seal contained both the cross and the rose —whence the term " Rosicrucian." The generally accepted theory regards the pamphlets as a sort of elaborate hoax perpetrated by Valentine Andrea, a young and benevolent Lutheran divine; but more, however, than a mere hoax. As the late Mr. R. A. Vaughan wrote : " . . . this Andrea writes the *Discovery of the Rosicrucian Brotherhood*, a *jeu-d'esprit* with a serious purpose, just as an experiment to see whether something cannot be done by combined effort to remedy the defect and abuses—social, educational, and religious, so lamented by all good men. He thought there were many Andreas scattered throughout Europe—how powerful would be their united systematic action ! . . . He hoped that the few nobler minds whom he desired to organize would see through the veil of fiction in which he had invested his proposal ; that he might communicate personally with some such, if they should appear ; or that his book might lead them to form among themselves a practical philanthropic confederacy, answering to the serious purpose he had embodied in his fiction." [2] His scheme was a

[2] ROBERT ALFRED VAUGHAN, B.A. : *Hours with the Mystics* (7th edition, 1895), vol. ii. bk. 8, chap. ix. p. 134.

failure, and on seeing its result, Andrea, not daring
to reveal himself as the author of the pamphlets, did
his best to put a stop to the folly by writing several
works in criticism of the Society and its claims.　Mr.
A. E. Waite, however, whose work on the subject
should be consulted for further information, rejects
this theory, and suggests that the Rosicrucian Society
was probably identical with the *Militia Crucifera
Evangelica*, a secret society founded in Nuremburg by
the Lutheran alchemist and mystic, Simon Studion.[3]

§ **50**. We must now turn our attention to the lives
and teachings of the alchemists of the period under
consideration, treating them, as far as
possible, in chronological order ; whence
the first alchemist to come under our
notice is Thomas Charnock.

Thomas
Charnock
(1524–1581).

Thomas Charnock was born at Faversham (Kent),
either in the year 1524 or in 1526.　After some
travels over England he settled at Oxford, carrying
on experiments in Alchemy.　In 1557 he wrote his
Breviary of Philosophy.　This work is almost entirely
autobiographical, describing Charnock's alchemistic
experiences.　He tells us that he was initiated into
the mysteries of the Hermetic Art by a certain James
S. of Salisbury ; he also had another master, an old
blind man, who instructed Charnock on his death-bed.
Unfortunately, however, Thomas was doomed to
failure in his experiments.　On the first attempt his
apparatus caught fire and his work was destroyed.
His next experiments were ruined by the negligence
of a servant.　His final misfortune shall be described

[3] ARTHUR EDWARD WAITE : *The Real History of the Rosicrucians*,
(1887).

in his own words. He had started the work for a third time, and had spent much money on his fire, hoping to be shortly rewarded. . . .

" Then a *Gentlemen* that oughte me great mallice
  Caused me to be prest to goe serve at *Callys :*
  When I saw there was no other boote,
  But that I must goe spight of my heart roote ;
  In my fury I tooke a Hatchet in my hand,
  And brake all my Worke whereas it did stand." ⁴

Thomas Charnock married in 1562 a Miss Agnes Norden. He died in 1581. It is, perhaps, unnecessary to say that his name does not appear in the history of Chemistry.

§ 51. **Andreas Libavius** was born at Halle in Germany in 1540, where he studied medicine and practiced for a short time as a physician.

Andreas Libavius (1540–1616.) He accepted the fundamental iatro-chemical doctrines, at the same time, however, criticising certain of the more extravagant views expressed by Paracelsus. He was a firm believer in the transmutation of the metals, but his own activities were chiefly directed to the preparation of new and better medicines. He enriched the science of Chemistry by many valuable discoveries, and tin tetra-chloride, which he was the first to prepare, is still known by the name of *spiritus fumans Libavii*. Libavius was a man possessed of keen powers of observation ; and his work on Chemistry, which contains a full account of the knowledge of the science of his time, may be

⁴ THOMAS CHARNOCK : *The Breviary of Naturall Philosophy* (see *Theatrum Chemicum Britannicum*, edited by Ashmole, 1652, p. 295.)

regarded as the first text-book of Chemistry.   It was held in high esteem for a considerable time, being reprinted on several occasions.

§ **52. Edward Kelley** or Kelly (see plate 9) was born at Worcester on August 1, 1555.   His life

Edward Kelley (1555–1595)

a John : ee (1527 -1608)

is so obscured by various traditions that it is very difficult to arrive at the truth concerning it.   The latest, and probably the best, account will be found in Miss Charlotte Fell Smith's *John Dee* (1909).   Edward Kelley, according to some accounts, was brought up as an apothecary.[5]   He is also said to have entered Oxford University under the pseudonym of Talbot.[6]   Later, he practised as a notary in London.   He is said to have committed a forgery, for which he had his ears cropped ; but another account, which supposes him to have avoided this penalty by making his escape to Wales, is not improbable.   Other crimes of which he is accused are coining and necromancy.   He was probably not guilty of all these crimes, but that he was undoubtedly a charlatan and profligate the sequel will make plain. We are told that about the time of his alleged escape to Wales, whilst in the neighbourhood of Glastonbury Abbey, he became possessed, by a lucky chance, of a manuscript by St. Dunstan setting forth the grand secrets of Alchemy, together with some of the two transmuting tinctures, both white and red,[7]

---

[5] See, for example, WILLIAM LILLY : *History of His Life and Times* (1715, reprinted in 1822, p. 227).

[6] See ANTHONY À WOOD's account of Kelley's life in *Athenæ Oxonienses* (3rd edition, edited by Philip Bliss, vol. i. col. 639.)

[7] William Lilly, the astrologer, in his *History of His Life and*

which had been discovered in a tomb near by. His
friendship with John Dee, or Dr. Dee as he is
generally called, commenced in 1582. Now, **John
Dee** (see plate 9) was undoubtedly a mathematician
of considerable erudition. He was also an astrologer,
and was much interested in experiments in "crystal-
gazing," for which purpose he employed a speculum of
polished cannel-coal, and by means of which he believed
that he had communication with the inhabitants of
spiritual spheres. It appears that Kelley, who probably did possess some mediumistic powers, the results
of which he augmented by means of fraud, interested
himself in these experiments, and not only became the
doctor's "scryer," but also gulled him into the belief
that he was in the possession of the arch-secrets of
Alchemy. In 1583, Kelley and his learned dupe left
England together with their wives and a Polish
nobleman, staying firstly at Cracovia and afterwards
at Prague, where it is not unlikely that the Emperor
Rudolph II. knighted Kelley. As instances of the
belief which the doctor had in Kelley's powers as
an alchemist, we may note that in his Private Diary
under the date December 19, 1586, Dee records that
Kelley performed a transmutation for the benefit of
one Edward Garland and his brother Francis;[8] and

Times (1822 reprint, pp. 225–226), relates a different story regarding
the manner in which Kelley is supposed to have obtained the Great
Medicine, but as it is told at third hand, it is of little importance.
We do not suppose that there can be much doubt that the truth
was that Dee and others were deceived by some skilful conjuring
tricks, for whatever else Kelley may have been, he certainly was a
very ingenious fellow.

[8] *The Private Diary of Dr. John Dee* (The Camden Society,
1842), p. 22.

PORTRAIT OF JOHN DEE.

PORTRAIT OF EDWARD KELLEY.

To face page 68]

under the date May 10, 1588, we find the following
recorded: "E.K. did open ʰthe great secret to me,
God be thanked!"⁹   That he was not always without
doubts as to Kelley's honesty, however, is evident
from other entries in his Diary.   In 1587 occurred an
event which must be recorded to the partners' lasting
shame.   To cap his former impositions, Kelley informed the doctor that by the orders of a spirit which
had appeared to him in the crystal, they were to share
"their two wives in common";   to which arrangement, after some further persuasion, Dee consented.
Kelley's profligacy and violent temper, however, had
already been the cause of some disagreement between
him and the doctor, and this incident leading to a
further quarrel, the erstwhile friends parted.   In 1589,
the Emperor Rudolph imprisoned Kelley, the price
of his freedom being the transmutative secret, or a
substantial quantity of gold, at least, prepared by its
aid.   He was, however, released in 1593; but died in
1595; according to one account, as the result of an
accident incurred while attempting to escape from a
second imprisonment.   Dee merely records that he
received news to the effect that Kelley "was
slayne."

It was during his incarceration that he wrote an
alchemistic work entitled *The Stone of the Philosophers*, which consists largely of quotations from
older alchemistic writings.   His other works on
Alchemy were probably written at an earlier period.[10]

⁹ *The Private Diary of Dr. John Dee* (The Camden Society,
1842), p. 27.

¹⁰ An English translation of Kelley's alchemistic works were published under the editorship of Mr. A. E. Waite, in 1893.

§ **53. Henry Khunrath** was born in Saxony in the second half of the sixteenth century. He was a follower of Paracelsus, and travelled about Germany, practising as a physician. "This German alchemist," says Mr. A. E. Waite, ". . . is claimed as a hierophant of the psychic side of the *magnum opus*, and . . . was undoubtedly aware of the larger issues of Hermetic theorems"; he describes Khunrath's chief work, *Amphitheatrum Sapientiæ Æternæ*, &c., as "purely mystical and magical."[11]

Henry Khunrath (1560–1605).

§ **54.** The date and birthplace of **Alexander Sethon,** a Scottish alchemist, do not appear to have been recorded, but **Michael Sendivogius** was probably born in Moravia about 1566. Sethon, we are told, was in possession of the arch-secrets of Alchemy. He visited Holland in 1602, proceeded after a time to Italy, and passed through Basle to Germany; meanwhile he is said to have performed many transmutations. Ultimately arriving at Dresden, however, he fell into the clutches of the young Elector, Christian II., who, in order to extort his secret, cast him into prison, and put him to the torture, but without avail. Now, it so happened that Sendivogius, who was in quest of the Philosopher's Stone, was staying at Dresden, and hearing of Sethon's imprisonment obtained permission to visit him. Sendivogius offered to effect Sethon's escape in return for assistance in his alchemistic pursuits, to which arrangement the Scottish alchemist willingly agreed. After some considerable outlay of money in bribery, Sen-

A e n ler S th n (?–1604) and Michael end1 ogiu (1566 ?–1646)

[11] A. E. WAITE: *Lives of Alchemystical Philosophers* (1888), p. 159.

divogius's plan of escape was successfully carried out,
and Sethon found himself a free man; but he refused
to betray the high secrets of Hermetic philosophy to
his rescuer. However, before his death, which occurred shortly afterwards, he presented him with an
ounce of the transmutative powder. Sendivogius soon
used up this powder, we are told, in effecting transmutations and cures, and, being fond of expensive
living, he married Sethon's widow, in the hope that
she was in the possession of the transmutative secret.
In this, however, he was disappointed; she knew
nothing of the matter, but she had the manuscript of
an alchemistic work written by her late husband.
Shortly afterwards Sendivogius printed at Prague a
book entitled *The New Chemical Light* under the name
of " Cosmopolita," which is said to be this work of
Sethon's but which Sendivogius claimed for his own
by the insertion of his name on the title-page, in the
form of an anagram. The tract *On Sulphur* which was
printed at the end of this book, however, is said
to have been the genuine work of the Moravian.
Whilst his powder lasted, Sendivogius travelled about,
performing, we are told, many transmutations. He
was twice imprisoned in order to extort the secrets of
Alchemy from him, on one occasion escaping, and on
the other occasion obtaining his release from the
Emperor Rudolph. Afterwards, he appears to have
degenerated into an impostor, but this is said to
have been a *finesse* to hide his true character as an
alchemistic adept. He died in 1646.[12]

The *New Chemical Light* was held in great
esteem by the alchemists. The first part treats at

[12] See F. B. : *Lives of Alchemystical Philosophers* (1815), pp.66–69.

length of the generation of the metals and also of the Philosopher's Stone, and claims to be based on practical experience. The seed of Nature, we are told, is one, but various products result on account of the different conditions of development. An imaginary conversation between Mercury, an Alchemist and Nature which is appended, is not without a touch of humour. Says the Alchemist, in despair, " Now I see that I know nothing ; only I must not say so. For I should lose the good opinion of my neighbours, and they would no longer entrust me with money for my experiments. I must therefore go on saying that I know everything ; for there are many that expect me to do great things for them. . . . There are many countries, and many greedy persons who will suffer themselves to be gulled by my promises of mountains of gold. Thus day will follow day, and in the meantime the King or the donkey will die, or I myself." [13] The second part treats of the Elements and Principles (see §§ 17 and 19).

§ **55. Michael Maier** (see plate 10) was born at Rendsberg (in Holstein) about 1568. He studied medicine assiduously, becoming a most Michael Maier (1568–1622). successful physician, and he was ennobled by Rudolf II. Later on, however, he took up the subject of Alchemy, and is said to have ruined his health and wasted his fortune in the pursuit of the alchemistic *ignis fatuus* —the Stone of the Philosophers—travelling about Germany and elsewhere in order to have converse with those who were regarded as adepts in the

[13] *The New Chemical Light*, Part I. (see *The Hermetic Museum*, vol. ii. p. 125).

PLATE 10.

TRES SCHOLA, TRES COESAR TITVLOS DE-
DIT; HÆC MIHI RESTANT,
POSSE BENE IN CHRISTO VIVERE, POSSE MORI.
MICHAEL MAIERVS COMES IMPERIALIS CON-
SISTORII etc: PHILOSOPH. ET MEDICINARVM
DOCTOR, P. C C NOBIL. EXEMPTVS FOR OLIM
MEDICVS CÆS: etc:

[by J. Brunn]

PORTRAIT OF
MICHAEL MAIER.

Art. He took a prominent part in the famous Rosicrucian controversy (see § 49), defending the claims
of the alleged society in several tracts. He is said,
on the one hand, to have been admitted as a member
of the fraternity; and on the other hand, to have
himself founded a similar institution. A full account
of his views will be found in the Rev. J. B. Craven's
Count Michael Maier: Life and Writings (1910).
He was a very learned man, but his works are somewhat obscure and abound in fanciful allegories. He
read an alchemistic meaning into the ancient fables
concerning the Egyptian and Greek gods and heroes.
Like most alchemists, he held the supposed virtues of
mercury in high esteem. In his *Lusus Serius : or,
Serious Passe-time*, for example, he supposes a Parliament of the various creatures of the world to meet, in
order that Man might choose the noblest of them
as king over all the rest. The calf, the sheep, the
goose, the oyster, the bee, the silkworm, flax and
mercury are the chosen representatives, each of
which discourses in turn. It will be unnecessary to
state that Mercury wins the day. Thus does Maier
eulogise it : " Thou art the miracle, splendour and
light of the world. Thou art the glory, ornament,
and supporter of the Earth. Thou art the Asyle,
Anchor, and tye of the Universe. Next to the minde
of Man, God Created nothing more Noble, more
Glorious, or more Profitable." [14] His *Subtle Allegory
concerning the Secrets of Alchemy, very useful to
possess and pleasant to read*, will be found in the
Hermetic Museum, together with his *Golden Tripod*,

[14] MICHAEL MAIER : *Lusus Serius : or Serious Passe-time* (1654),
p. 138.

consisting of translations of " Valentine's " "*Practica* " and *Twelve Keys*, Norton's *Ordinal* and Cremer's spurious *Testament*.

§ **56. Jacob Boehme,** or Behmen (see plate 11), was born at Alt Seidenberg, a village near Gorlitz, in 1575. His parents being poor, the education he received was of a very rudimentary nature, and when his schooling days were over, Jacob was apprenticed to a shoemaker. His religious nature caused him often to admonish his fellow-apprentices, which behaviour ultimately caused him to be dismissed. He travelled about as a journeyman shoemaker, returning, however, to Gorlitz in 1594, where he married and settled in business. He claims to have experienced a wonderful vision in 1598, and to have had a similar vision two years later. In these visions, the first of which lasted for several days he believed that he saw into the inmost secrets of nature ; but what at first appeared dim and vague became clear and coherent in a third vision, which he tells us was vouchsafed to him in 1610. It was then that he wrote his first book, the *Aurora*, which he composed for himself only, in order that he should not forget the mysteries disclosed to him. At a later period he produced a large number of treatises of a mystical-religious nature, having spent the intervening years in improving his early education. These books aroused the ire of the narrow-minded ecclesiastical authorities of the town, and Jacob suffered considerable persecution in consequence. He visited Dresden in 1624, and in the same year was there taken ill with a fever, returning to Gorlitz, where he expired in a condition of ecstasy.

Jacob Boehme
(1575–1624.)

PLATE II.

PORTRAIT OF
JACOB BOEHME.

Jacob Boehme was an alchemist of a purely transcendental order. He had, it appears, acquired some knowledge of Chemistry during his apprentice days, and he employed the language of Alchemy in the elaboration of his system of mystical philosophy. With this lofty mystical-religious system we cannot here deal ; Boehme is, indeed, often accounted the greatest of true Christian mystics ; but although conscious of his superiority over many minor lights, we think this title is due to Emanuel Swedenborg. The question of the validity of his visions is also one which lies beyond the scope of the present work ; [15] we must confine our attention to Boehme as an alchemist. The Philosopher's Stone, in Boehme's terminology, is the Spirit of Christ which must "tincture" the individual soul. In one place he says, " The *Phylosophers Stone* is a very dark disesteemed Stone, of a *Gray* colour, but therein lyeth the highest Tincture." [16] In the transcendental sense, this is reminiscent of the words of Isaiah : " He hath no form nor comeliness ; and when we see him, there is no beauty that we should desire him. . . . He was despised and we esteemed him not," &c. [17]

§ **57. John Baptist van Helmont** (see plate 12) was born in Brussels in 1577. He devoted himself to the study of medicine, at first following Galen, but

[15] For a general discussion of spiritual visions see the present writer's *Matter, Spirit and the Cosmos* (Rider, 1910), Chapter IV., " On Matter and Spirit." Undoubtedly Boehme's visions involved a valuable element of truth, but at the same time much that was purely relative and subjective.

[16] JACOB BOEHME : *Epistles* (translated by J. E., 1649), Ep. iv. § 111, p. 65.

[17] *The Book of the Prophet Isaiah*, chap. liii., vv. 2 and 3, R.V.

afterwards accepting in part the teachings of Paracelsus ; and he helped to a large extent in the overthrow of the old medical doctrines. His purely chemical researches were also of great value to the science. He was a man of profound knowledge, of a religious temperament, and he possessed a marked liking for the mystical. He was inspired by the writings of Thomas a Kempis to imitate Christ in all things, and he practised medicine, therefore, as a work of benevolence, asking no fee for his services. At the same time, moreover, he was a firm believer in the powers of the Philosopher's Stone, claiming to have himself successfully performed the transmutation of the metals on more than one occasion, though unacquainted with the composition of the medicine employed (see § 62). Many of his theoretical views are highly fantastical. He lived a life devoted to scientific research, and died in 1644.

J. B. van Helmont (1577–1644) and F. M. van m (1618–1699)

Van Helmont regarded water as the primary element out of which all things are produced. He denied that fire was an element or anything material at all, and he did not accept the sulphur-mercury-salt theory. To him is due the word "gas"—before his time various gases were looked upon as mere varieties of air—and he also made a distinction between gases (which could not be condensed) [18] and vapours (which give liquids on cooling). In particular he investigated the gas that is now known as carbon-dioxide (carbonic anhydride), which he termed *gas sylvestre;* but he lacked suitable apparatus for the

[18] It has since been discovered that all gases can be condensed, given a sufficient degree of cold and pressure.

PLATE 12.

PORTRAITS OF

J. B. AND F. M. VAN HELMONT.

(From the Frontispiece to J. B. van Helmont's *Oriatrike.*)

collection of gases, and hence was led in many cases to erroneous conclusions.

Francis Mercurius van Helmont (see plate 12), the son of John Baptist, born in 1618, gained the reputation of having also achieved the *magnum opus*, since he appeared to live very luxuriously upon a limited income. He was a skilled chemist and physician, but held many queer theories, metempsychosis included.

§ 58. Johann Rudolf Glauber was born at Karlstadt in 1604. Of his life little is known. He appears to have travelled about Germany a good
Johann Rudolf Glauber (1604–1668). deal, afterwards visiting Amsterdam, where he died in 1668. He was of a very patriotic nature, and a most ardent investigator in the realm of Chemistry. He accepted the main iatro-chemical doctrines, but gave most of his attention to applied Chemistry. He enriched the science with many important discoveries; and crystallised sodium sulphate is still called "Glauber's Salt." Glauber, himself, attributed remarkable medicinal powers to this compound. He was a firm believer in the claims of Alchemy, and held many fantastic ideas.

§ 59. Thomas Vaughan, who wrote under the name of **"Eugenius Philalethes,"** was born at Newton in Brecknockshire in 1622. He was edu-
Thomas Vaughan ("Eugenius P. a. hes") (1622–1666.) cated at Jesus College, Oxford, graduating as a Bachelor of Arts, and being made a fellow of his college. He appears also to have taken holy orders and to have had the living of St. Bridget's (Brecknockshire) conferred on him.[19]

[19] See ANTHONY A WOOD: *Athenæ Oxonienses*, edited by Philip Bliss, vol. iii. (1817), cols. 722–726.

During the civil wars he bore arms for the king, but his allegiance to the Royalist cause led to his being accused of "drunkenness, swearing, incontinency and bearing arms for the King"; and he appears to have been deprived of his living. He retired to Oxford and gave himself up to study and chemical research. He is to be regarded as an alchemist of the transcendental order. His views as to the nature of the true Philosopher's Stone may be gathered from the following quotation: "This, reader," he says, speaking of the mystical illumination, "is the Christian Philosopher s Stone, a Stone so often inculcated in Scripture. This is the Rock in the wildernesse, because in great obscurity, and few there are that know the right way unto it. This is the Stone of Fire in Ezekiel; this is the Stone with Seven Eyes upon it in Zacharie, and this is the White Stone with the New Name in the Revelation. But in the Gospel, where Christ himself speakes, who was born to discover mysteries and communicate Heaven to Earth, it is more clearly described."[20] At the same time he appears to have carried out experiments in physical Alchemy, and is said to have met with his death in 1666 through accidentally inhaling the fumes of some mercury with which he was experimenting.

Thomas Vaughan was an ardent disciple of Cornelius Agrippa, the sixteenth-century theosophist. He held the peripatetic philosophy in very slight esteem. He was a man devoted to God, though probably guilty of some youthful follies, full of love

[20] THOMAS VAUGHAN ("Eugenius Philalethes"): *Anima Magica Abscondita* (see *The Magical Writings of Thomas Vaughan*, edited by A. E. Waite, 1888, p. 71).

towards his wife, and with an intense desire for the solution of the great problems of Nature. Amongst his chief works, which are by no means wanting in flashes of mystic wisdom, we may mention *Anthroposophia Theomagica*, *Anima Magica Abscondita* (which were published together), and *Magia Adamica ; or, the Antiquitie of Magic*. With regard to his views as expressed in the first two of these books, a controversy ensued between Vaughan and Henry Moore, which was marked by considerable acrimony.

§ **60**. The use of the pseudonym " Philalethes " has not been confined to one alchemist. The cosmopolitan adept who wrote under the name of **"Eirenæus Philalethes,"** has been confused, on the one hand, with Thomas Vaughan, on the other hand with George Starkey (?–1665). His real identity remains shrouded in impenetrable mystery. **George Starkey,** who graduated M.A. at Harvard in 1646, probably made the acquaintance of the mysterious adept whilst practising medicine in the United States of America, and was to some extent initiated by him into the secrets of Alchemy. In return for this he appears to have stolen his Hermetic master's MS., *The Marrow of Alchemy*, which he published in 1654–5. Returning to England, Starkey seems to have degenerated into a quack.[21] The works of " Eirænius Philalethes," which are among the most lucid of alchemistic writings, became immensely popular. His *Open Entrance to the Closed Palace of the King* (the most famous of his works) and his *Three*

Side note: "Eirenæus Philalethes" (1623 ?– ?) and George Starkey (?–1665).

[21] See **Mr.** A. E. Waite's *Lives of Alchemystical Philosophers*, article, " Eirenæus Philalethes."

Treatises will be found in *The Hermetic Museum.*
Some of his views we have already noted (see
§§ 1 and 22). On certain points he differed from
the majority of the alchemists. He denied that fire
was an element, and, also, that bodies are formed by
mixture of the elements. According to him there is
one principle in the metals, namely, mercury, which
arises from the aqueous element, and is termed
"metalically differentiated water, *i.e.,* it is water
passed into that stage of development, in which it can
no longer produce anything but mineral substances."[22]
Philalethes's views as to "metallic seed" are also of
considerable interest. Of the seed of gold, which he
regarded as the seed, also, of all other metals, he says:
"The seed of animals and vegetables is something
separate, and may be cut out, or otherwise separately
exhibited; but metallic seed is diffused throughout
the metal, and contained in all its smallest parts;
neither can it be discerned from its body: its extraction is therefore a task which may well tax the
ingenuity of the most experienced philosopher. . . ."[23]
There appears to be somewhat of a similarity between
this view of the seed of metals and modern ideas
regarding the electron (see §§ 80 and 81), which must
not be passed over without notice.

[22] "EIRENÆUS PHILALETHES": *The Metamorphosis of Metals*
(see *The Hermetic Museum*, vol. ii. p. 236). Compare with van
Helmont's views, § 57.

[23] "EIRENÆUS PHILALETHES": *The Metamorphosis of Metals*
(see *The Hermetic Museum*, vol. ii. p. 240).

CHAPTER V

THE OUTCOME OF ALCHEMY

§ **61.** The alchemists were untiring in their search for the Stone of the Philosophers, and we may well

Did the Alchemists achieve the "Magnum Opus"? ask whether they ever succeeded in effecting a real transmutation. That many *apparent* transmutations occurred, the observers being either self-deceived by a superficial examination—certain alloys resemble the " noble metals " — or deliberately cheated by impostors, is of course undoubted. But at the same time we must not assume that, because we know not the method now, real transmutations have never taken place. Modern research indicates that it may be possible to transmute other metals (more especially silver) into gold, and consequently we must admit the possibility that amongst the many experiments carried out, a real transmutation was effected. On the other hand, the method which is suggested by the recent researches in question could not possibly have been known to the alchemists or accidentally employed by them ; and, moreover, the quantity of gold which is hoped for, should such a method prove successful, is far below the smallest amount that would have been detected in

the days of Alchemy.   But if there be one method
whereby the metals may be transmuted, there may be
other methods.   And it is not altogether an easy task
to explain away the testimony of eminent men such
as were van Helmont and Helvetius.

§ 62. John Baptist van Helmont (see § 57), who
was celebrated alike for his skill as a physician and
chemist and for his nobility of character,

The Testi-
mony of van
Helmont.

testified in more than one place that he
had himself carried out the transmutation
of mercury into gold.   But, as we have
mentioned above, the composition of the Stone employed on these occasions was unknown to him.   He
says : " . . . For truly, I have divers times seen it
[the Stone of the Philosophers], and handled it with
my hands : but it was of colour, such as is in Saffron
in its Powder, yet weighty, and shining like unto
powdered Glass : There was once given unto me
one fourth part of one Grain : But I call a Grain the
six hundredth part of one Ounce : This quarter of
one Grain therefore, being rouled up in Paper, I projected upon eight Ounces of Quick-silver made hot in
a Crucible ; and straightway all the Quick-silver, with
a certain degree of Noise, stood still from flowing, and
being congealed, setled like unto a yellow Lump : but
after pouring it out, the Bellows blowing, there were
found eight Ounces, and a little less than eleven Grains
[eight Ounces less eleven Grains] of the purest Gold :
Therefore one only Grain of that Powder, had transchanged 19186 [19156] Parts of Quick-silver, equal
to itself, into the best Gold." [1]

[1] J. B. VAN HELMONT : *Life Eternal* (see *Oriatrike*, translated by
J. C., 1662 ; or *Van Helmont's Workes*, translated by J. C., 1664,

And again: "I am constrained to believe that there is the Stone which makes Gold, and which makes Silver; because I have at distinct turns, made projection with my hand, of one grain of the Powder, upon some thousand grains of hot Quick-silver; and the buisiness succeeded in the Fire, even as Books do promise; a Circle of many People standing by, together with a tickling Admiration of us all. . . . He who first gave me the Gold-making Powder, had likewise also, at least as much of it, as might be sufficient for changing two hundred thousand Pounds of Gold: . . . For he gave me perhaps half a grain of that Powder, and nine ounces and three quarters of Quick-silver were thereby transchanged: But that Gold, a strange man [a stranger], being a Friend of one evenings acquaintance, gave me."[2]

§ **63. John Frederick Helvetius** (see plate 13), an eminent doctor of medicine, and physician to the Prince of Orange, published at the Hague in 1667 the following remarkable account of a transmutation he claimed to have effected. Certain points of resemblance between this account and that of van Helmont (*e.g.*, in each case the Stone is described as a glassy substance of a pale yellow colour) are worth noticing: "On the 27 December, 1666, in the forenoon, there came to my house a certain man, who was a complete stranger to me, but of an honest, grave countenance, and an authoritative

The Testimony of Helvetius.

which is merely the former work with a new title-page and preliminary matter, pp. 751 and 752).

[2] J. B. VAN HELMONT: *The Tree of Life* (see *Oriatrike* or *Van Helmont's Workes*, p. 807).

mien, clothed in a simple garb like that of a Mem-
nonite . . .

"After we had exchanged salutations, he asked me
whether he might have some conversation with me.
He wished to say something to me about the Pyro-
technic Art, as he had read one of my tracts (directed
against the sympathetic Powder of Dr. Digby), in
which I hinted a suspicion whether the Grand Arcanum
of the Sages was not after all a gigantic hoax. He,
therefore, took that opportunity of asking me whether
I could not believe that such a grand mystery might
exist in the nature of things, by means of which a
physician could restore any patient whose vitals were
not irreparably destroyed. I answered : 'Such a
Medicine would be a most desirable acquisition for
any physician ; nor can any man tell how many secrets
there may be hidden in Nature ; yet, though I have
read much about the truth of this Art, it has never
been my good fortune to meet with a real Master of
the Alchemical Science.' I also enquired whether he
was a medical man. . . . In reply, he . . . described
himself as a brassfounder. . . . After some further
conversation, the Artist Elias (for it was he) thus
addressed me : 'Since you have read so much in the
works of the Alchemists about this Stone, its substance, its colour, and its wonderful effects, may I be
allowed the question, whether you have not yourself
prepared it ?' On my answering his question in the
negative, he took out of his bag a cunningly-worked
ivory box, in which there were three large pieces of
a substance resembling glass, or pale sulphur, and
informed me that here was enough of the Tincture
for the production of 20 tons of gold. When I

PLATE 13.

IOHANNES FRIDERICUS HELVETIUS,
ANHALTINUS COTHONENSIS DOCTOR a/q;
Pracucus Meaicinæ HAGÆ COMITIS. ÆT. 30. Aᵒ. 166;.
Contra vim Mortis est panacea. Radix Iesse mea Iesu.

had held the precious treasure in my hand for a quarter of an hour (during which time I listened to a recital of its wonderful curative properties), I was compelled to restore it to its owner, which I could not help doing with a certain degree of reluctance. After thanking him for his kindness in shewing it to me, I then asked how it was that his Stone did not display that ruby colour, which I had been taught to regard as characteristic of the Philosopher's Stone. He replied that the colour made no difference, and that the substance was sufficiently mature for all practical purposes. My request that he would give me a piece of his Stone (though it were no larger than a coriander seed), he somewhat brusquely refused, adding, in a milder tone, that he could not give it me for all the wealth I possessed, and that not on account of its great preciousness, but for some other reason which it was not lawful for him to divulge ; . . .

§ **64.** " When my strange visitor had concluded his narrative, I besought him to give me a proof of his assertion, by performing the transmutatory operation on some metals in my presence. He answered evasively, that he could not do so then, but that he would return in three weeks, and that, if he was then at liberty to do so, he would shew me something that would make me open my eyes. He appeared punctually to the promised day, and invited me to take a walk with him, in the course of which we discoursed profoundly on the secrets of Nature in fire, though I noticed that my companion was very chary in imparting information about the Grand Arcanum. . . . At last I asked him point-blank to show me

Helvetius obtains the Philosopher's Stone.

the transmutation of metals.   I besought him to come
and dine with me, and to spend the night at my house;
I entreated ; I expostulated ; but in vain.   He remained
firm.   I reminded him of his promise.   He retorted
that his promise had been conditional upon his being
permitted to reveal the secret to me.   At last, however, I prevailed upon him to give me a piece of his
precious Stone—a piece no larger than a grain of
rape seed.   He delivered it to me as if it were the
most princely donation in the world.   Upon my utter-
ing a doubt whether it would be sufficient to tinge
more than four grains of lead, he eagerly demanded
it back.   I complied, in the hope that he would ex-
change it for a larger piece ; instead of which he
divided it in two with his thumb, threw away one-half
and gave me back the other, saying : ' Even now it
is sufficient for you.'   Then I was still more heavily
disappointed, as I could not believe that anything
could be done with so small a particle of the Medicine.
He, however, bade me take two drachms, or half an
ounce of lead, or even a little more, and to melt it
in the crucible ; for the Medicine would certainly not
tinge more of the base metal than it was sufficient for.
I answered that I could not believe that so small a
quantity of Tincture could transform so large a mass
of lead.   But I had to be satisfied with what he had
given me, and my chief difficulty was about the application of the Tincture.   I confessed that when I held
his ivory box in my hand, I had managed to extract
a few crumbs of his Stone, but that they had changed
my lead, not into gold, but only into glass.   He
laughed, and said that I was more expert at theft
than at the application of the Tincture.   ' You should

have protected your spoil with "yellow wax," then it would have been able to penetrate the lead and to transmute it into gold.' . . .

§ **65**. ". . . With . . . a promise to return at nine o'clock the next morning, he left me. But at the stated hour on the following day he did not make his appearance; in his stead, however, there came, a few hours later, a stranger, who told me that his friend the Artist was unavoidably detained, but that he would call at three o'clock in the afternoon. The afternoon came; I waited for him till half-past seven o'clock. He did not appear. Thereupon my wife came and tempted me to try the transmutation myself. I determined, however, to wait till the morrow, and in the meantime, ordered my son to light the fire, as I was now almost sure that he was an impostor. On the morrow, however, I thought that I might at least make an experiment with the piece of 'Tincture' which I had received; if it turned out a failure, in spite of my following his directions closely, I might then be quite certain that my visitor had been a mere pretender to a knowledge of this Art. So I asked my wife to put the Tincture in wax, and I myself, in the meantime, prepared six drachms of lead; I then cast the Tincture, enveloped as it was in wax, on the lead; as soon as it was melted, there was a hissing sound and a slight effervescence, and after a quarter of an hour I found that the whole mass of lead had been turned into the finest gold. Before this transmutation took place, the compound became intensely green, but as soon as I had poured it into the melting pot it assumed a hue like blood. When it cooled, it glittered

Helvetius performs a Transmutation.

and shone like gold. We immediately took it to the goldsmith, who at once declared it to be the finest gold he had ever seen, and offered to pay fifty florins an ounce for it.

§ **66.** "The rumour, of course, spread at once like wildfire through the whole city ; and in the afternoon, I had visits from many illustrious students

Gold Assayed. of this Art, I also received a call from the Master of the Mint and some other gentlemen, who requested me to place at their disposal a small piece of the gold, in order that they might subject it to the usual tests. I consented, and we betook ourselves to the house of a certain silversmith, named Brechtil, who submitted a small piece of my gold to the test called 'the fourth': three or four parts of silver are melted in the crucible with one part of gold, and then beaten out into thin plates, upon which some strong *aqua fortis* [nitric acid] is poured. The usual result of this experiment is that the silver is dissolved, while the gold sinks to the bottom in the shape of a black powder, and after the *aqua fortis* has been poured off, [the gold,] melted once again in the crucible, resumes its former shape. . . . When we now performed this experiment, we thought at first that one-half of the gold had evaporated; but afterwards we found that this was not the case, but that, on the contrary, two scruples of the silver had undergone a change into gold.

§ **67.** "Then we tried another test, *viz.*, that which is performed by means of a septuple of Antimony; at first it seemed as if eight grains of the gold had been lost, but afterwards, not only had two scruples of the silver been converted into gold, but the silver itself was greatly improved both in quality and malleability. Thrice I performed this infallible test, discovering that every drachm of gold produced an increase of a scruple of gold, but the silver is excellent and extremely flexible. Thus I have unfolded to you the whole story from beginning to end. The gold I still retain in my possession, but I cannot tell you what has become of the Artist Elias. Before he left me, on the last day of our friendly intercourse, he told me that he was on the point of undertaking a journey to the Holy Land. May the Holy Angels of God watch over him wherever he is, and long preserve him as a source of blessing to Christendom! This is my earnest prayer on his and our behalf." [3]

Helvetius's Gold Further Tested.

Testimony such as this warns us not to be too sure that a real transmutation has never taken place. On the whole, with regard to this question, an agnostic position appears to be the more philosophical.

§ **68**. But even if the alchemists did not discover the Grand Arcanum of Nature, they did discover very many scientifically important facts. Even if they did not prepare the Philosopher's Stone, they did prepare a very large number of new and important chemical compounds. Their labours were the seeds out of which modern Chemistry developed, and this highly important science is rightfully included under the expression " The Outcome of Alchemy." As we have already pointed out (§ 48), it was the iatro-chemists who first investigated chemical matters with an object other than alchemistic,

The Genesis of Chemistry.

[3] J. F. HELVETIUS: *The Golden Calf*, ch. iii. (see *The Hermetic Museum*, vol. ii. pp. 283 *et. seq.*).

their especial end in view being the preparation of useful medicines, though the medical-chemist and the alchemist were very often united in the one person, as in the case of Paracelsus himself and the not less famous van Helmont.   It was not until still later that Chemistry was recognised as a distinct science separate from medicine.

§ **69.** In another direction the Outcome of Alchemy was of a very distressing nature.   Alchemy was in many respects eminently suitable as a cloak for fraud, and those who became "alchemists" with the sole object of accumulating much wealth in a short space of time, finding that the legitimate pursuit of the Art did not enable them to realise their expectations in this direction, availed themselves of this fact. There is, indeed, some evidence that the degeneracy of Alchemy had commenced as early as the fourteenth century, but the attainment of the *magnum opus* was regarded as possible for some three or more centuries.

The alchemistic promises of health, wealth and happiness and a pseudo-mystical style of language were effectively employed by these impostors.   Some more or less ingenious tricks—such as the use of hollow stirring-rods, in which the gold was concealed, &c.— convinced a credulous public of the validity of their claims.   Of these pseudo-alchemists we have already mentioned Edward Kelley and George Starkey, but chief of them all is generally accounted the notorious "Count Cagliostro."   That Cagliostro is rightfully placed in the category of pseudo-alchemists is certain, but it also appears equally certain that, charlatan though he was, posterity has not always done him

The Degeneracy of Alchemy.

that justice which is due to all men, however bad they may be.

§ **70.** Of the birth and early life of the personage calling himself "**Count Cagliostro**" nothing is known with any degree of certainty, even his true name being enveloped in mystery. It has, indeed, been usual to identify him with the notorious Italian swindler, Giuseppe Balsamo, who, born at Palermo in 1743 (or 1748), apparently disappeared from mortal ken after some thirty years, of which the majority were spent in committing various crimes. "Cagliostro's" latest biographer,[4] who appears to have gone into the matter very thoroughly, however, throws very grave doubts on the truth of this theory.

"Count Cagliostro" *? 1795*.

If the earlier part of "Cagliostro's" life is unknown, the latter part is so overlaid with legends and lies, that it is almost impossible to get at the truth concerning it. In 1776 Cagliostro and his wife were in London, where "Cagliostro" became a Freemason, joining a lodge connected with "The Order of Strict Observance," a secret society incorporated with Freemasonry,

[4] W. R. H. TROWBRIDGE: *Cagliostro: The Splendour and Misery of a Master of Magic* (1910). We must acknowledge our indebtedness for many of the particulars which follow to this work. It is, however, unfortunately marred by a ridiculous attempt to show a likeness between "Cagliostro" and Swedenborg, for which, by the way, Mr. Trowbridge has already been criticised by the *Spectator*. It may justly be said of Swedenborg that he was scrupulously honest and sincere in his beliefs as well as in his actions; and, as a philosopher, it is only now being discovered how really great he was. He did, indeed, claim to have converse with spiritual beings; but the results of modern psychical research have robbed such claims of any inherent impossibility, and in Swedenborg's case there is very considerable evidence in the validity of his claims.

and which (on the Continent, at least) was concerned largely with occult subjects. "Cagliostro," however, was unsatisfied with its rituals and devised a new system which he called Egyptian Masonry. Egyptian Masonry, he taught, was to reform the whole world, and he set out, leaving England for the Continent, to convert Masons and others to his views. We must look for the motive power of his extraordinary career in vanity and a love of mystery-mongering, without any true knowledge of the occult ; it is probable, indeed, that ultimately his unbounded vanity triumphed over his reason and that he actually believed in his own pretensions. That he did possess hypnotic and clair-voyant powers is, we think, at least probable ; but it is none the less certain that, when such failed him, he had no scruples against employing other means of convincing the credulous of the validity of his claims. This was the case on his visit to Russia, which occurred not long afterwards. At St. Petersburg a youthful medium he was employing, to put the matter briefly, "gave the show away," and at Warsaw, where he found it necessary to turn alchemist, he was detected in the process of introducing a piece of gold in the crucible containing the base metal he was about to "transmute." At Strasburg, which he reached in 1780, however, he was more successful. Here he appeared as a miraculous healer of all diseases, though whether his cures are to be ascribed to some simple but efficacious medicine which he had dis-covered, to hypnotism, to the power of the imagina-tion on the part of his patients, or to the power of imagination on the part of those who have recorded the alleged cures, is a question into which we do not

PLATE 14.

COMTE de CAGLIOSTRO.

'ace page 92]

propose to enter.   At Strasburg "Cagliostro" came into contact with the Cardinal de Rohan, and a fast friendship sprang up between the two, which, in the end, proved "Cagliostro's" ruin.   The "Count" next visited Bordeaux and Lyons, successfully founding lodges of Egyptian Masonry.   From the latter town he proceeded to Paris, where he reached the height of his fame.   He became extraordinarily rich, although he is said to have asked, and to have accepted, no fee for his services as a healer.   On the other hand, there was a substantial entrance-fee to the mysteries of Egyptian Masonry, which, with its alchemistic promises of health and wealth, prospered exceedingly.   At the summit of his career, however, fortune forsook him.   As a friend of de Rohan, he was arrested in connection with the Diamond Necklace affair, on the word of the infamous Countess de Lamotte ; although, of whatever else he may have been guilty, he was perfectly innocent of this charge.   After lying imprisoned in the Bastille for several months, he was tried by the French Parliament, pronounced innocent, and released.   Immediately, however, the king banished him, and he left Paris for London, where he seems to have been persistently persecuted by agents of the French king. He returned to the Continent, ultimately reaching Italy, where he was arrested by the Inquisition and condemned to death on the charge of being a Freemason (a dire offence in the eyes of the Roman Catholic Church).   The sentence, however, was modified to one of perpetual imprisonment, and he was confined in the Castle of San Leo, where he died in 1795, after four years of imprisonment, in what manner is not known.

CHAPTER VI

THE AGE OF MODERN CHEMISTRY

§ **71.** Chemistry as distinct from Alchemy and Iatro-chemistry commenced with Robert Boyle (see plate 15), who first clearly recognised that its aim is neither the transmutation of the metals nor the preparation of medicines, but the observation and generalisation of a certain class of phenomena ; who denied the validity of the alchemistic view of the constitution of matter, and enunciated the definition of an element which has since reigned supreme in Chemistry ; and who enriched the science with observations of the utmost importance. Boyle, however, was a man whose ideas were in advance of his times, and intervening between the iatro-chemical period and the Age of Modern Chemistry proper came the period of the Phlogistic Theory—a theory which had a certain affinity with the ideas of the alchemists.

The Birth of Modern Chemistry.

§ **72.** The phlogiston theory was mainly due to Georg Ernst Stahl (1660–1734). Becher (1635–1682) had attempted to revive the once universally accepted sulphur-mercury-salt theory of the alchemists in a somewhat modified form, by the assumption that all substances consist of three earths—the

PLATE 15.

G. Vertue del. t Sculp.t 1739.   In the Collection of Dr. Mead   Impensis J.&P. Knapton Londini 1740.   J. Kerseboom pinx.t

PORTRAIT OF ROBERT BOYLE.

combustible, mercurial, and vitreous ; and herein is to be found the germ of Stahl's phlogistic theory.

The Phlogiston Theory. According to Stahl, all combustible bodies (including those metals that change on heating) contain *phlogiston*, the principle of combustion, which escapes in the form of flame when such substances are burned. According to this theory, therefore, the metals are compounds, since they consist of a metallic calx (what we now call the "oxide" of the metal) combined with phlogiston ; and, further, to obtain the metal from the calx it is only necessary to act upon it with some substance rich in phlogiston. Now, coal and charcoal are both almost completely combustible, leaving very little residue ; hence, according to this theory, they must consist very largely of phlogiston ; and, as a matter of fact, metals can be obtained by heating their calces with either of these substances. Many other facts of a like nature were explicable in terms of the phlogiston theory, and it became exceedingly popular. Chemists at this time did not pay much attention to the balance ; it was observed, however, that metals increased in weight on calcination, but this was "explained" on the assumption that phlogiston possessed negative weight. Antoine Lavoisier (1743–1794), utilising Priestley's discovery of oxygen (called "dephlogisticated air" by its discoverer) and studying the weight relations accompanying combustion, demonstrated the non-validity of the phlogistic theory[1] and proved combustion to be the combination of the substance burnt

---

[1] It should be noted, however, that if by the term "phlogiston" we were to understand energy and not some form of matter, most of the statements of the phlogistics would be true so far as they go.

with a certain constituent of the air, the oxygen.   By
this time Alchemy was to all intents and purposes
defunct, Boerhave (1668–1738) was the last eminent
chemist to give any support to its doctrines, and the
new chemistry of Lavoisier gave it a final death-blow.
We now enter upon the Age of Modern Chemistry,
but we shall deal in this chapter with the history
of chemical theory only so far as is necessary in
pursuance of our primary object, and hence our
account will be very far from complete.

§ **73.** Robert Boyle (1626–1691) had defined an
element as a substance which could not be decomposed, but which could enter into combi-
Boyle and the nation with other elements giving com-
of an Element. pounds capable of decomposition into
these original elements.   Hence, the
metals were classed among the elements, since they
had defied all attempts to decompose them.   Now, it
must be noted that this definition is of a negative
character, and, although it is convenient to term
"elements" all substances which have so far defied
decomposition, it is a matter of impossibility to decide
what substances are true elements with absolute
certainty; and the possibility, however faint, that
gold and other metals are of a compound nature, and
hence the possibility of preparing gold from the
"base" metals or other substances, must always
remain.   This uncertainty regarding the elements
appears to have generally been recognised by the
new school of chemists, but this having been so, it is
the more surprising that their criticism of alchemistic
art was not less severe.

74. With the study of the relative weights in

which substances combine, certain generalisations or "natural laws" of supreme importance were discovered. These stoichiometric laws, as they are called, are as follows :—

The Stoichiometric Laws.

1. "The Law of Constant Proportion"— *The same chemical compound always contains the same elements, and there is a constant ratio between the weights of the constituent elements present.*

2. "The Law of Multiple Proportions"—*If two substances combine chemically in more than one proportion, the weights of the one which combine with a given weight of the other, stand in a simple rational ratio to one another.*

3. "The Law of Combining Weights"—*Substances combine either in the ratio of their combining numbers, or in simple rational multiples or submultiples of these numbers.* (The weights of different substances which combine with a given weight of some particular substance, which is taken as the unit, are called the combining numbers of such substances with reference to this unit. The usual unit now chosen is 8 grammes of Oxygen.)[2]

As examples of these laws we may take the few following simple facts :—

---

[2] In order that these laws may hold good, it is, of course, necessary that the substances are weighed under precisely similar conditions. To state these laws in a more absolute form, we can replace the term "weight" by "mass," or in preference, "inertia"; for the inertias of bodies are proportional to their weights, providing that they are weighed under precisely similar conditions. For a discussion of the exact significance of these terms "mass" and "inertia," the reader is referred to the present writer's *Matter, Spirit and the Cosmos* (Rider, 1910), Chapter I., "On the Doctrine of the Indestructibility of Matter."

1. Pure water is found always to consist of oxygen and hydrogen combined in the ratio of 1·008 parts by weight of the latter to 8 parts by weight of the former; and pure sulphur-dioxide, to take another example, is found always to consist of sulphur and oxygen combined in the ratio of 8·02 parts by weight of sulphur to 8 parts by weight of oxygen. (The Law of Constant Proportion.)

2. Another compound is known consisting only of oxygen and hydrogen, which, however, differs entirely in its properties from water. It is found always to consist of oxygen and hydrogen combined in the ratio of 1·008 parts by weight of the latter to 16 parts by weight of the former, i.e., in it a definite weight of hydrogen is combined with an amount of oxygen *exactly twice* that which is combined with the same weight of hydrogen in water. No definite compound has been discovered with a constitution intermediate between these two. Other compounds consisting only of sulphur and oxygen are also known. One of these (viz., sulphur-trioxide, or sulphuric anhydride) is found always to consist of sulphur and oxygen combined in the ratio of 5·35 parts by weight of sulphur to 8 parts by weight of oxygen. We see, therefore, that the weights of sulphur combined with a definite weight of oxygen in the two compounds called respectively "sulphur-dioxide" and "sulphur-tri-oxide," are in the proportion of 8·02 to 5·35, i.e., 3 : 2. Similar simple ratios are obtained in the case of all the other compounds. (The Law of Multiple Proportions.)

3. From the data given in (1) above we can fix the combining number of hydrogen as 1·008, that of

sulphur as 8·02. Now, compounds are known containing sulphur and hydrogen, and, in each case, the weight of sulphur combined with 1·008 grammes of hydrogen is found always to be either 8·02 grammes or some multiple or submultiple of this quantity. Thus, in the simplest compound of this sort, containing only hydrogen and sulphur (viz., sulphuretted-hydrogen or hydrogen sulphide), 1·008 grammes of hydrogen is found always to be combined with 16·04 grammes of sulphur, *i.e.*, exactly twice the above quantity. (The Law of Combining Weights.)

Berthollet (1748–1822) denied the truth of the law of constant proportion, and hence, of course, the other stoichiometric laws, and a controversy ensued between this chemist and Proust (1755–1826), who undertook a research to settle the question and in whose favour the controversy was ultimately decided.

§ **75.** At the beginning of the nineteenth century, John Dalton (see plate 15) put forward his Atomic Theory in explanation of these facts. This theory assumes (1) that all matter is made up of small indivisible and indestructible particles, called "atoms"; (2) that all atoms are *not* alike, there being as many different sorts of atoms as there are elements; (3) that the atoms constituting any one element are exactly alike and are of definite weight; and (4) that compounds are produced by the combination of different atoms. Now, it is at once evident that if matter be so constituted, the stoichiometric laws must necessarily follow. For the smallest particle of any definite compound (now called a "molecule") must consist of a definite assemblage of different atoms, and these

Dalton's Atomic Theory.

atoms are of definite weight : whence the law of
constant proportion.   One atom of one substance may
combine with 1, 2, 3 . . . atoms of some other substance, but it cannot combine with some fractional part
of an atom, since the atoms are indivisible : whence
the law of multiple proportions.   And these laws
holding good, and the atoms being of definite weight,
the law of combining weights necessarily follows.
Dalton's Atomic Theory gave a simple and intelligible
explanation of these remarkable facts regarding the
weights of substances entering into chemical combination, and, therefore, gained universal acceptance.   But
throughout the history of Chemistry can be discerned
a spirit of revolt against it as an explanation of the
absolute constitution of matter.   The tendency of
scientific philosophy has always been towards Monism
as opposed to Dualism, and here were not merely two
eternals, but several dozen ; Dalton's theory denied
the unity of the Cosmos, it lacked the unifying
principle of the alchemists.   It is only in recent times
that it has been recognised that a scientific hypothesis
may be very useful without being altogether true.
As to the usefulness of Dalton's theory there can be
no question ; it has accomplished that which no other
hypothesis could have done ; it rendered the concepts
of a chemical element, a chemical compound and a
chemical reaction definite ; and has, in a sense, led to
the majority of the discoveries in the domain of
Chemistry that have been made since its enunciation.
But as an expression of absolute truth, Dalton's
theory, as is very generally recognised nowadays, fails
to be satisfactory.   In the past, however, it has been
the philosophers of the materialistic school of thought,

PLATE 16.

Allen, Pinx^t   Cook, Sc.

PORTRAIT OF JOHN DALTON.

rather than the chemists *qua* chemists, who have insisted on the absolute truth of the Atomic Theory; Kekulé, who by developing Franklin's theory of atomicity or valency[3] made still more definite the atomic view of matter, himself expressed grave doubts as to the absolute truth of Dalton's theory; but he regarded it as *chemically* true, and thus voices what appears to be the opinion of the majority of chemists nowadays, namely, there are such things as chemical atoms and chemical elements, incapable of being decomposed by purely chemical means, but that such are not absolute atoms or absolute elements, and

[3] The term "valency" is not altogether an easy one to define; we will, however, here do our best to make plain its significance. In a definite chemical compound we must assume that the atoms constituting each molecule are in some way bound together (though not, of course, rigidly), and we may speak of "bonds" or "links of affinity," taking care, however, not to interpret such terms too literally. Now, the number of "affinity links" which one atom can exert is not unlimited; indeed, according to the valency theory as first formulated, it is fixed and constant. It is this number which is called the "valency" of the element; but it is now known that the "valency" in most cases can vary between certain limits. Hydrogen, however, appears to be invariably univalent, and is therefore taken as the unit of valency. Thus, Carbon is quadrivalent in the methane-molecule, which consists of one atom of carbon combined with four atoms of hydrogen; and Oxygen is divalent in the water-molecule, which consists of one atom of oxygen combined with two atoms of hydrogen. Hence, we should expect to find one atom of carbon combining with two of oxygen, which is the case in the carbon-dioxide—(carbonic anhydride) — molecule. The underlying reason of this regularity remains unknown (see § 81), and there are very many curious exceptions to it. For a development of the thesis, so far as the compounds of carbon are concerned, that each specific "affinity link" corresponds in general to a definite and constant amount of energy, which is evolved as heat on disruption of the bond, the reader is referred to the present writer's monograph *On the Calculation of Thermo-Chemical Constants* (Arnold, 1909).

consequently not impervious to all forms of action. But of this more will be said later.

§ **76.** With the acceptance of Dalton's Atomic Theory, it became necessary to determine the atomic weights of the various elements, *i.e.*, not the absolute atomic weights, but the relative weights of the various atoms with reference to one of them as unit.4 We cannot in this place enter upon a discussion of the various difficulties, both of an experimental and theoretical nature, which were involved in this problem, save to remark that the correct atomic weights could be arrived at only with the acceptance of Avogadro's Hypothesis. This hypothesis, which is to the effect that equal volumes of different gases measured at the same temperature and pressure contain an equal number of gaseous molecules, was put forward in explanation of a number of facts connected with the physical behaviour of gases; but its importance was for some time unrecognised, owing to the fact that the distinction between atoms and molecules was not yet clearly drawn. A list of those chemical substances at present recognised as " elements," together with their atomic weights, will be found on pp. 106, 107.

§ **77.** It was observed by a chemist of the name of Prout, that, the atomic weight of hydrogen being taken

(margin note) The Determination of the Atomic Weights of the Elements.

4 Since hydrogen is the lightest of all known substances, the unit, Hydrogen = 1, was at one time usually employed. However, it was seen to be more convenient to express the atomic weights in terms of the weight of the oxygen-atom, and the unit, Oxygen = 16 is now always employed. This value for the oxygen-atom was chosen so that the approximate atomic weights would in most cases remain unaltered by the change.

as the unit, the atomic weights of nearly all the elements approximated to whole numbers; and in 1815

Prout's Hypothesis. he suggested as the reason for this regularity, that all the elements consist solely of hydrogen. Prout's Hypothesis received on the whole a very favourable reception; it harmonised Dalton's Theory with the grand concept of the unity of matter—all matter was hydrogen in essence; and Thomas Thomson undertook a research to demonstrate its truth. On the other hand, however, the eminent Swedish chemist, Berzelius, who had carried out many atomic weight determinations, criticised both Prout's Hypothesis and Thomson's research (which latter, it is true, was worthless) in most severe terms; for the hypothesis amounted to this— that the decimals in the atomic weights obtained experimentally by Berzelius, after so much labour, were to be regarded as so many errors. In 1844, Marignac suggested half the hydrogen atom as the unit, for the element chlorine, with an atomic weight of 35·5, would not fit in with Prout's Hypothesis as originally formulated; and later, Dumas suggested one-quarter. With this theoretical division of the hydrogen-atom, the hypothesis lost its simplicity and charm, and was doomed to downfall. Recent and most accurate atomic weight determinations show clearly that the atomic weights are not exactly whole numbers, but that, nevertheless, the majority of them (if expressed in terms of $O = 16$ as the unit) do approximate very closely to such. The Hon. R. J. Strutt has recently calculated that the probability of this occurring, in the case of certain of the commoner elements, by mere chance is exceedingly small (about 1 in

1,000.)⁵ Several hypotheses attempting to explain this very remarkable fact have been put forward, but its real significance still remains unknown.⁶

⁵ Hon. R. J. STRUTT: "On the Tendency of the Atomic Weights to approximate to Whole Numbers," *Philosophical Magazine* [6], vol. i. (1901), pp. 311 *et seq.*

⁶ Two examples of these attempts must here suffice. Mr. A. C. G. Egerton ("The Divergence of the Atomic Weights of the Lighter Elements from Whole Numbers," *Journal of the Chemical Society*, vol. xcv. pp. 238 *et seq.*, 1909) finds that the atomic weights ($H = 1$) of the lighter elements (up to Phosphorus) can be calculated with considerable accuracy by means of the formulæ—

(i) $M = 2N \pm 0.0078 \times 2N$ and   (ii) $M = 2N + 1 \pm 0.0078 \times 2N$,

where M is the atomic weight, and N the number of the element, reckoning Helium as 2, Lithium as 3, and so on, the elements being numbered in the order of their atomic weights. The first formula applies in the case of "even" elements, the second in the case of "odd" elements. For elements of higher atomic weight, similar but more complicated formulæ were found for those with atoms not heavier than Cobalt. Beyond Cobalt the method does not appear to be applicable. The author suggests that, since the figure 0.0078 represents approximately the weight of a group of eight electrons (see below, §§ 79 and 80), the elements may be built up of conglomerates of hydrogen atoms with groups of eight or sixteen electrons added or subtracted. But, as he remarks at the close of his paper (p. 242), "The physical interpretation of the relation given is evidently not the only one that can be devised. Since the elements are built up by the conglomeration of the fundamental stuff, although not necessarily evolved in order of atomic weight, and since the atoms probably differ in internal structure, there are certain to be changes in the internal energy of the atoms causing slight differences in mass. One would expect such changes to be proportional to the increase of the amount of the original stuff which conglomerates; the formula $M = A \pm A \,(0.0078)$ $[A = 2N]$ agrees with this idea; and, further, it is conceivable that an increase in the size of an atom, due to addition of more matter, and the formation of a new atom, might either cause an increase or decrease of energy according to the configuration of the new atom; the positive and negative sign in the formula might thus be explained."

§ **78.** A remarkable property of the atomic weights was discovered, in the sixties, independently by Lothar Meyer and Mendeleeff. They

The "Periodic Law"

found that the elements could be arranged in rows in the order of their atomic weights so that similar elements would be found in the same columns. A modernised form of the Periodic Table will be found on pp. 106, 107. It will be noticed, for example, that the "alkali" metals, Lithium, Sodium, Rubidium and Cæsium, which

Dr. James Moir ("A Method of Harmonising the Atomic Weights," *Journal of the Chemical Society*, vol. xcv. pp. 1752 *et seq.*, 1909) criticises the above-mentioned paper. He assumes (p. 1752) "the cause of valency, at all events the fundamental valency of each element, to be the presence, in varying numbers, of a sub-element of atomic weight $\frac{1}{112}$ [= ·0089]. . . . If this be denoted by μ, then the univalent elements contain 1μ, the bivalent 2μ, the tervalent 3μ, and so on. In addition, the author conceives the main bulk of the mass of the elements to be due to polymerisation of an entity consisting of the hydrogen atom less the aggregation μ. Denoting this by $\bar{H}$, we have, for example: $H = \bar{H} + \mu$; $Li = 7\bar{H} + \mu$; $C = 12\bar{H} + 4\mu$; $O = 16\bar{H} + 2\mu$; $Ne = 20\bar{H}$; $Na = 23\bar{H} + \mu$; $Ag = 108\bar{H} + \mu$; $Cs = 133\bar{H} + \mu$." The atomic weights calculated on these assumptions are in excellent agreement with the experimental. Thus—

$$H + \mu = H = 1·0078,$$

therefore

$\bar{H} = 1·0078 - ·0089 - ·9989.$
$Li = 7\bar{H} + \mu = 7·001$ (Experimental value = 6·94)
$O = 16\bar{H} + 2\mu = 16·000$ (Experimental value = 16·00)
$Ne = 20\bar{H} = 19·978$ (Experimental value = 20·2), &c.

However, there are some elements which do not fit into this scheme, and whose atomic weights can be calculated by this method only by employing multiples of $\bar{H}$ involving one decimal figure (for example, Chlorine and Sulphur), which elements the author regards as not being direct polymerides of $\bar{H}$.

THE PERIODIC TABLE OF THE CHEMICAL ELEMENTS.

	0	1	2	3	4	5	6	7	8
	Helium He = 3·99	[Hydrogen][a] [H = 1·008]						Hydrogen H = 1·008	
	Neon Ne = 20·2	Lithium Li = 6·94	Glucinum Gl = 9·1	Boron B = 11·0	Carbon C = 12·00	Nitrogen N = 14·01	Oxygen O = 16·00	Fluorine F = 19·0	
	Argon A = 39·88	Sodium Na = 23·00	Magnesium Mg = 24·32	Aluminium Al = 27·1	Silicon Si = 28·3	Phosphorus P = 31·04	Sulphur S = 32·07	Chlorine Cl = 35·46	
		Potassium[b] K = 39·10	Calcium Ca = 40·09	Scandium Sc = 44·1	Titanium Ti = 48·1	Vanadium V = 51·06	Chromium Cr = 52·0	Manganese Mn = 54·93	Iron Fe = 55·85[c] Cobalt Co = 58·97 Nickel Ni = 58·68
	Krypton Kr = 82·9	Copper Cu = 63·57	Zinc Zn = 65·37	Gallium Ga = 69·9	Germanium Ge = 72·5	Arsenic As = 74·96	Selenium Se = 79·2	Bromine Br = 79·92	
		Rubidium Rb = 85·45	Strontium Sr = 87·63	Yttrium Y = 89·0	Zirconium Zr = 90·6	Columbium Cb = 93·5	Molybdenum Mo = 96·0	?	Ruthenium Ru = 101·7 Rhodium Rh = 102·9 Palladium Pd = 106·7
		Silver Ag = 107·88	Cadmium Cd = 112·40	Indium In = 114·8	Tin Sn = 119·0	Antimony Sb = 120·2	Tellurium Te = 127·5	Iodine[d] I (or J) = 126·92	

Xenon Xe=130·2	?	?	Emanation (Niton) 222·4
Caesium Cs=132·81	?	Gold Au=197·2	?
Barium Ba=137·37	?	Mercury Hg=200·0	Radium Ra=226·4
Lanthanum La=139·0	?	Thallium Tl=204·0	?
Cerium Ce=140·25	?	Lead Pb=207·10	Thorium Th=232·0
?	Tantalum Ta=181·0	Bismuth Bi=208·0	?
?	Tungsten W=184·0	?	Uranium U=238·5
?	?	?	?
?	Osmium Os=190·9, Iridium Ir=193·1, Platinum Pt=195·2	?	?

NOTES.

There re sp al somewhat different forms of this Periodic Table. This is one of the simplest, but it lacks certain advantages of son of the more complicated forms. The atomic weights given are those of the International Atomic Weights Committee for 1911. They are calculated on the basis, Oxygen = 16. The number of decimal places given in each case indicates the degree of accuracy with which each atomic weight has been determined. The letter or letters underneath the name of each element is the symbol by which it is invariably designated by chemists.

The number above each column indicates the valency which the elements of each group exhibit towards oxygen. Many of the elements are exceptional in this respect.

* The exact position of Hydrogen is in dispute.

† The positions of Argon and Potassium have been inverted, in order that these elements may fall in the right columns with the elements they resemble; and so have the positions of Tellurium and iodine

‡ The whole of "Group 8" forms an exception to the Table.

§ There are a number o ill-defined rare earth metals with atomic weights lying between those of Cerium and Tantalum. They all appear to resemble the elements of "Group 3," so that their position in the Table cannot be decided with accuracy.

resemble one another very closely, fall in Column 1 ; the "alkaline earth" metals occur together in Column 2 ; though in each case these are accompanied by certain elements with somewhat different properties. Much the same holds good in the case of the other columns of this Table; there is manifested a remarkable regularity, with certain still more remarkable divergences (see notes appended to Table on pp. 106, 107). This regularity exhibited by the " elements " is of considerable importance, since it shows that, in general, the properties of the " elements " are *periodic* functions of their atomic weights ; and, together with certain other remarkable properties of the " elements," distinguishes them sharply from the " compounds." It may be concluded with tolerable certainty, therefore, that if the " elements " are in reality of a compound nature, they are all, in general, compounds of a like nature distinct from that of other compounds.

It is now some years since Sir William Crookes first attempted to explain the periodicity of the properties of the elements on the theory that they have all been evolved by a conglomerating process from some primal stuff—the protyle—consisting of very small particles. He represents the action of this generative cause by means of a " figure of eight " spiral, along which the elements are placed at regular intervals, so that similar elements come underneath one another, as in Mendeleeff s table, though the grouping differs in some respects. The slope of the curve is supposed to represent the decline of some factor (*e.g.*, temperature) conditioning the process, which process is assumed to be of a recurrent nature, like the swing of a pendulum. After the completion of one swing (to keep to the illustration of a pendulum) whereby one series of elements is produced, owing to the decline of the above-mentioned factor, the same series of elements is not again the result as would otherwise be the case, but a somewhat different series is produced, each member of which resembles the corresponding member of the former series. Thus, if the first series contains, for example, helium, lithium, carbon, &c., the second series will contain instead, argon, potassium, titanium, &c. The whole theory, though highly interesting, is, however, by no means free from defects.

§ **79.** We must now turn our attention to those recent views of the constitution of matter which

Th
Corpuscular
Theory of
matter.

originated to a great extent in the investigations of the passage of electricity through gases at very low pressures. It will be possible, however, on the present occasion, to give only the very briefest account of the subject; but a fuller treatment is rendered unnecessary by the fact that these and allied investigations and the theories to which they have given rise have been fully treated in several well-known works, by various authorities on the subject, which have appeared during the last few years.[7]

When an electrical discharge is passed through a high-vacuum tube, invisible rays are emitted from the kathode, generally with the production of a greenish-

---

[7] We have found Prof. Harry Jones' *The Electrical Nature of Matter and Radioactivity* (1906), Mr. Soddy's *Radioactivity* (1904), and Mr. Whetham's *The Recent Development of Physical Science* (1909) particularly interesting. Mention, of course, should also be made of the standard works of Prof. Sir J. J. Thomson and Prof. Rutherford.

yellow fluorescence where they strike the glass walls of the tube. These rays are called " kathode rays." At one time they were regarded as waves in the ether, but it was shown by Sir William Crookes that they consist of small electrically charged particles, moving with a very high velocity. Sir J. J. Thomson was able to determine the ratio of the charge carried by these particles to their mass or inertia ; he found that this ratio was constant whatever gas was contained in the vacuum tube, and much greater than the corresponding ratio for the hydrogen ion (electrically charged hydrogen atom) in electrolysis. By a skilful method, based on the fact discovered by Mr. C. T. R. Wilson, that charged particles can serve as nuclei for the condensation of water-vapour, he was further able to determine the value of the electrical charge carried by these particles, which was found to be constant also, and equal to the charge carried by univalent ions, *e.g.*, hydrogen, in electrolysis. Hence, it follows that the mass of these kathode particles must be much smaller than the hydrogen ion, the actual ratio being about 1 : 1700. The first theory put forward by Sir J. J. Thomson in explanation of these facts, was that these kathode particles ("corpuscles" as he termed them) were electrically charged portions of matter, much smaller than the smallest atom ; and since the same sort of corpuscle is obtained whatever gas is contained in the vacuum tube, it is reasonable to conclude that the corpuscle is the common unit of all matter.

§ 80. This eminent physicist, however, had shown mathematically that a charged particle moving with a very high velocity (approaching that of light) would exhibit an appreciable increase in mass or inertia due to the charge, the magnitude of such inertia depending on the velocity of the particle. This was

Proof that
the Electrons
are not
Ma er.

experimentally verified by Kaufmann, who determined the velocities, and the ratios between the electrical charge and the inertia, of various kathode particles and similar particles which are emitted by compounds of radium (see §§ 89 and 90). Sir J. J. Thomson calculated these values on the assumption that the inertia of such particles is entirely of electrical origin, and thereby obtained values in remarkable agreement with the experimental. There is, therefore, no reason for supposing the corpuscle to be matter at all; indeed, if it were, the above agreement would not be obtained. As Professor Jones says: "Since we know things only by their properties, and since all the properties of the corpuscle are accounted for by the electrical charge associated with it, why assume that the corpuscle contains anything but the electrical charge? It is obvious that there is no reason for doing so.

"*The corpuscle is, then, nothing but a disembodied electrical charge*, containing nothing material, as we have been accustomed to use that term. It is electricity, and nothing but electricity. With this new conception a new term was introduced, and, now, instead of speaking of the corpuscle we speak of the *electron*"[8] Applying this modification to the above view of the constitution of matter, we have what is called "the electronic theory," namely, that the

[8] H. C. JONES: *The Electrical Nature of Matter and Radioactivity* (1906), p. 21.

material atoms consist of electrons, or units of electricity in rapid motion; which amounts to this—that matter is simply an electrical phenomenon.

§ 81. Sir J. J. Thomson has elaborated this theory of the nature and constitution of matter; he has shown what systems of electrons would be stable, and has attempted to find therein the significance of Mendeléeff's generalisation and the explanation of valency.

The Electronic Theory of ɯa er.

There can be no doubt that there is a considerable element of truth in the electronic theory of matter; the one characteristic property of matter, *i.e.*, inertia, can be accounted-for electrically; but further than this it is not yet possible to say. The fundamental difficulty is that the electrons are units of negative electricity, whereas matter is electrically neutral. Is there a positive electron? Professor Sir J. J. Thomson assumes a sphere or shell of positive electrification wherein the (negative) electrons revolve; and to this positive electricity, it seems, must be ascribed the major portion of the inertia or mass of the atom, for recent work has proved that the number of electrons in an atom is approximately equal to the atomic weight of that atom as expressed in terms of $H = 1$ or $O = 16$ as unit. This fact has rather discountenanced the corpuscular and electronic theories of matter, which as originally formulated assumed the whole mass of the atom to be due alone to corpuscles or electrons, and, therefore, required the atoms to contain thousands of such units; but, as Professor Sir J. J. Thomson has pointed out, it is not really incompatible therewith, if, as does not seem unlikely, all mass is really mass of the ether of space (see next section).9 The whole question, however, cannot be regarded as finally settled ; but it is hoped that further research will throw light on the disputed points.

§ **82.** The analysis of matter has been carried a step further. A philosophical view of the Cosmos

The
Etheric
Theory of
ma er.

involves the assumption of an absolutely continuous and homogeneous medium filling all space, for an absolute vacuum is unthinkable, and if it were supposed that the stuff filling all space is of an atomic structure, the question arises, What occupies the interstices between its atoms? This ubiquitous medium is termed by the scientists of to-day "the Ether of Space." Moreover, such a medium as the Ether is demanded by the phenomena of light. It appears, however, that the ether of space has another and a still more important function than the transmission of light : the idea that matter has its explanation therein is being developed by Sir Oliver Lodge. The evidence certainly points to the conclusion that matter is some sort of singularity in the ether, probably a stress centre. We have been too much accustomed to think of the ether as something excessively light and quite the reverse of massive or dense, in which it appears we have been wrong. Sir Oliver Lodge calculates that the density of the ether is far greater than that of the most dense forms of matter ; not that matter is to be thought of as a rarefaction of the ether, for the ether within matter is as dense as that without. What we call matter, however, is not a continuous substance ; it consists,

9 See Professor Sir J. J. THOMSON : *The Corpuscular Theory of Matter* (1907), especially pp. 142 *et seq.*

rather, of a number of widely separated particles, whence its comparatively small density compared with the perfectly continuous ether. Further, if there is a difficulty in conceiving how a perfect fluid like the ether can give rise to a solid body possessed of such properties as rigidity, impenetrability and elasticity, we must remember that all these properties can be produced by means of motion. A jet of water moving with a sufficient velocity behaves like a rigid and impenetrable solid, whilst a revolving disc of paper exhibits elasticity and can act as a circular saw.[10]   It appears, therefore, that the ancient doctrine of the alchemistic essence is fundamentally true after all, that out of the "One Thing" all material things have been produced by adaptation or modification ; and, as we have already noticed (§ 60), there also appears to be some resemblance between the concept of the electron and that of the seed of gold, which seed, it should be borne in mind, was regarded by the alchemists as the common seed of all metals.

§ **83.** There are also certain other facts which appear to demand such a modification of Dalton's Atomic Theory as is found in the Electronic Theory. One of the characteristics of the chemical elements is that each one gives a spectrum peculiar to itself. The spectrum of an element must, therefore, be due to its atoms, which in some way are able, at a sufficiently high temperature, to act upon the ether so as to produce vibrations of definite and characteristic wave-length. Now, in many cases the number of lines of definite wave-

Further Evidence of the Complexity of the Atoms.

[10] See Sir OLIVER LODGE, F.R.S.: *The Ether of Space* (1909).

length observed in such a spectrum is considerable, for example, hundreds of different lines have been observed in the arc-spectrum of iron. But it is incredible that an atom, if it were a simple unit, would give rise to such a number of different and definite vibrations, and the only reasonable conclusion is that the atoms must be complex in structure. We may here mention that spectroscopic examination of various heavenly bodies leads to the conclusion that there is some process of evolution at work building up complex elements from simpler ones, since the hottest nebulæ appear to consist of but a few simple elements, whilst cooler bodies exhibit a greater complexity.

§ 84. Such modifications of the atomic theory as those we have briefly discussed above, although profoundly modifying, and, indeed, controverting the philosophical significance of Dalton's theory as originally formulated, leave its chemical significance

Views of Wald and Ostwald.

practically unchanged. The atoms can be regarded no longer as the eternal, indissoluble gods of Nature that they were once supposed to be ; thus, Materialism is deprived of what was thought to be its scientific basis.[11] But the science of Chemistry is unaffected thereby ; the atoms are not the ultimate units out of which material things are built, but the atoms cannot be decomposed by purely chemical means ; the "elements" are not truly elemental, but *they are chemical elements.* However, the atomic theory has been subjected to a far more searching criticism. Wald argues that substances obey the law of definite

[11] For a critical examination of Materialism, the reader is referred to the present writer's *Matter, Spirit and the Cosmos* (Rider, 1910), especially Chapters I. and IV.

proportions because of the way in which they are prepared; chemists refuse, he says, to admit any substance as a definite chemical compound unless it does obey this law. Wald's opinions have been supported by Professor Ostwald, who has attempted to deduce the other stoichiometric laws on these grounds without assuming any atomic hypothesis [12]; but these new ideas do not appear to have gained the approval of chemists in general. It is not to be supposed that chemists will give up without a struggle a mental tool of such great utility as Dalton's theory, in spite of its defects, has proved itself to be. There does seem, however, to be logic in the arguments of Wald and Ostwald, but it is too early in the history of the controversy to say what the ultimate result will be. So far as can be seen, however, it appears that, on the one hand, the atomic theory is not necessitated by the so-called "stoichiometric laws"; whilst, on the other hand, a molecular constitution of matter seems to be demanded by the phenomenon known as the "Brownian Movement," i.e., the spontaneous, irregular and apparently perpetual movement of microscopic portions of solid matter when immersed in a liquid medium; such movement appearing to be explicable only as the result of the motion of the molecules of which the liquid in question is built up.[13]

[12] W. OSTWALD : "Faraday Lecture," *Journal of the Chemical Society*, vol. lxxxv. (1904), pp. 506 *et seq.* See also W. OSTWALD : *The Fundamental Principles of Chemistry* (translated by H. W. Morse, 1909), especially Chapters VI., VII. and VIII.

[13] For an account of this singular phenomenon, see Prof. JEAN PERRIN : *Brownian Movement and Molecular Reality* (translated from the *Annales de Chimie et de Physique*, 8me Series, September, 1909, by F. Soddy, M.A., F.R.S., 1910).

CHAPTER VII

MODERN ALCHEMY

§ **85.** Correctly speaking, there is no such thing as " Modern Alchemy"; not that Mysticism is dead, or

" Modern Alchemy "
that men no longer seek to apply the principles of Mysticism to phenomena on the physical plane, but they do so after another manner from that of the alchemists. A new science, however, is born amongst us, closely related on the one hand to Chemistry, on the other to Physics, but dealing with changes more profound and reactions more deeply seated than are dealt with by either of these; a science as yet without a name, unless it be the not altogether satisfactory one of " Radioactivity." It is this science, or, perhaps we should say, a certain aspect of it, to which we refer (it may be fantastically) by the expression " Modern Alchemy": the aptness of the title we hope to make plain in the course of the present chapter.

§ **86.** As is commonly known, what are called X-rays are produced when an electric discharge is passed through a high-vacuum tube. It has been shown that these rays are a series of irregular pulses in the ether, which are set up when the kathode particles strike the walls of the glass vacuum tube,[1] and it was found that more powerful effects can be produced by inserting a disc of platinum in the path of the kathode particles. It was

X-rays and ̶B̶e̶c̶q̶u̶e̶r̶e̶l̶ rays. M Becquerel who first discovered that there are substances which naturally emit radiations similar to X-rays. He found that uranium compounds affected a photographic plate from which they were carefully screened, and he also showed that these uranium radiations, or "Becquerel rays," resemble X-rays in other particulars. It was already known that certain substances fluoresce (emit light) in the dark after having been exposed to sunlight, and it was thought at first that the above phenomenon exhibited by uranium salts was of a like nature, since certain uranium salts are fluorescent; but M. Becquerel found that uranium salts which had never been exposed to sunlight were still capable of affecting a photographic plate, and that this remarkable property was possessed by all uranium salts, whether fluorescent or not. This phenomenon is known as "radioactivity," and bodies which exhibit it are said to be "radioactive." Schmidt found that thorium compounds possess a similar property, and Professor Rutherford showed that thorium compounds evolved also something resembling a gas. He called this an "emanation."

§ **87.** Mme. Curie [2] determined the radioactivity of many uranium and thorium compounds, and found that there was a proportion between the radioactivity

---

[1] They must not be confused with the greenish-yellow phosphorescence which is also produced: the X-rays are invisible.

[2] See Madame SKLODOWSKA CURIE'S *Radio-active Substances* (2nd ed., 1904).

of such compounds and the quantity of uranium or thorium in them, with the remarkable exception of

T̶h̶e̶o̶r̶y̶ of Radium certain natural ores, which had a radio-activity much in excess of the normal, and, indeed, in certain cases, much greater than pure uranium. In order to throw some light on this matter, Mme. Curie prepared one of these ores by a chemical process and found that it possessed a normal radioactivity. The only logical conclusion to be drawn from these facts was that the ores in question must contain some unknown, highly radio-active substance, and the Curies were able, after very considerable labour, to extract from pitchblende (the ore with the greatest radioactivity) minute quanti-ties of the salts of two new elements—which they named " Polonium " and " Radium " respectively— both of which were extremely radioactive.

M. Debierne has obtained a third radioactive substance from pitchblende, which he has called " Actinium."

§ **88.** Radium is an element resembling calcium, strontium, and barium in chemical properties ; its

Chemical Pro-perties of Radium. atomic weight was determined by Mme. Curie, and found to be about 225, accord-ing to her first experiments ; a redeter-mination gave a slightly higher value, which has been confirmed by a further investigation carried out by Sir T. E. Thorpe.[3]   Radium gives a

---

[3] See Sir T. E. THORPE: "On the Atomic Weight of Radium" (Bakerian Lecture for 1907. Delivered before the Royal Society, June 20, 1907), *Proceedings of the Royal Society of London*, vol. lxxx. pp. 298 *et seq.* ; reprinted in *The Chemical News*, vol. xcvii. pp. 229 *et seq.* (May 15, 1908).

characteristic spectrum, and is intensely radioactive. It should be noted that up to the middle of the year 1910 the element radium itself had not been prepared; in all the experiments carried out radium salts were employed (*i.e.*, certain compounds of radium with other elements), generally radium chloride and radium bromide. More recently Mme. Curie, in conjunction with M. Debierne, has obtained the free metal. It is described as a white, shining metal resembling the other alkaline earth metals. It reacts very violently with water, chars paper with which it is allowed to come in contact, and blackens in the air, probably owing to the formation of a nitride. It fuses at 700° C., and is more volatile than barium.[4]

§ 89. Radium salts give off three distinct sorts of rays, referred to by the Greek letters a, β, γ. The a-rays have been shown to consist of

The Radio-activity of Radium. electrically charged (positive) particles, with a mass approximately equal to that of four hydrogen atoms; they are slightly deviated by a magnetic field, and do not possess great penetrative power. The β-rays are similar to the kathode rays, and consist of (negative) electrons; they are strongly deviated by a magnetic field, in a direction opposite to that in which the a-particles are deviated, and possess medium penetrative power, passing for the most part through a thin sheet of metal. The γ-rays resemble X-rays; they possess

[4] Madame P. CURIE and M. A. DEBIERNE: "Sur le radium metallique," *Comptes Rendus hebdomadaires des Seances l'Academie des Sciences*, vol. cli. (1910), pp. 523-525. (For an English translation of this paper see *The Chemical News*, vol. cii. p. 175.)

great penetrative power, and are not deviated by a magnetic field. The difference in the effect of the magnetic field on these rays, and the difference in their penetrative power, led to their detection and allows of their separate examination. Radium salts emit also an emanation, which tends to become occluded in the solid salt, but can be conveniently liberated by dissolving the salt in water, or by heating it. The emanation exhibits the characteristic properties of a gas, it obeys Boyle's Law (i.e., its volume varies inversely with its pressure), and it can be condensed to a liquid at low temperatures ; its density as determined by the diffusion method is about 100. Attempts to prepare chemical compounds of the emanation have failed, and in this respect it resembles the rare gases of the atmosphere—helium, neon, argon, krypton, and xenon—whence it is probable that its molecules are monatomic, so that a density of 100 would give its atomic weight as 200.5 As can be seen from the table on pp. 106, 107, an atomic weight of about 220 corresponds to a position in the column containing the rare gases in the periodic system. That the emanation actually has an atomic weight of these dimensions has been confirmed by further experiments recently carried out by Sir William Ramsay and Dr. R. W. Gray.[6] These chemists have determined the density of the emanation by actually weighing minute quantities of known volume of the substance, sealed up in small capillary tubes, a specially sensitive

[5] This follows from Avogadro's Hypothesis, see § 76.
[6] Sir WILLIAM RAMSAY and Dr. R. W. GRAY: "La densite de l'emanation du radium," *Comptes Rendus hebdomadaires des Seances de l'Académie des Sciences*, vol. cvi. (1910), pp. 126 et seq.

balance being employed. Values for the density varying from 108 to 113½, corresponding to values for the atomic weight varying from 216 to 227, were thereby obtained. Sir William Ramsay, therefore, considers that there can no longer be any doubt that the emanation is one of the elements of the group of chemically inert gases. He proposes to call it *Niton*, and, for reasons which we shall note later, considers that in all probability it has an atomic weight of 222½.

§ **90.** Radium salts possess another very remarkable property, namely, that of continuously emitting light and heat. It seemed, at first, that here was a startling contradiction to the law of the conservation of energy, but the whole mystery becomes comparatively clear in terms of the corpuscular or the electronic theory of matter. The radium-atom is a system of a large number (see § 81) of corpuscles or electrons, and contains in virtue of their motion an enormous amount of energy. But it is known from Chemistry that atomic systems (*i.e.*, molecules) which contain very much energy are unstable and liable to explode. The same law holds good on the more interior plane—the radium-atom is liable to, and actually does, explode. And the result? Energy is set free, and manifests itself partly as heat and light. Some free electrons are shot off (the β-rays), which, striking the undecomposed particles of salt, give rise to pulses in the ether (the γ-rays),[7] just as the kathode particles give rise to X-rays when they

The Disintegration of the Radium Atom.

---

[7] This view regarding the γ-rays is not, however, universally accepted, some scientists regarding them as consisting of a stream of particles moving with very high velocities.

strike the walls of the vacuum tube or a platinum disc placed in their path. The β and γ-rays do not, however, result immediately from the exploding radium-atoms, the initial products being the emanation and one α-particle from each radium-atom destroyed.

§ 91. Radium salts have the property of causing surrounding objects to become temporally radioactive. This "induced radioactivity," as it may "Induced Radioactivity." be called, is found to be due to the emanation, which is itself radioactive (it emits α-rays only), and is decomposed into minute traces of solid radioactive deposits. By examining the rate of decay of the activity of the deposit, it has been found that it is undergoing a series of sub-atomic changes, the products being termed Radium A, B, C, &c. It has been proved that all the β and γ-rays emitted by radium salts are really due to certain of these secondary products. Radium F is thought to be identical with Polonium (§ 87). Another product is also obtained by these decompositions, with which we shall deal later (§ 94).

§ 92. Uranium and thorium differ in one important respect from radium, inasmuch as the first product of the decomposition of the uranium and Properties of thorium atoms is in both cases solid. Thorium. Sir William Crookes [8] was able to separate from uranium salts by chemical means a small quantity of an intensely radioactive substance, which he called Uranium X, the residual uranium having lost most of its activity; and M.

[8] Sir WILLIAM CROOKES, F.R.S.: "Radio-activity of Uranium," *Proceedings of the Royal Society of London*, vol. lxvi. (1900), pp. 409 *et seq.*

Becquerel, on repeating the experiment, found that the activity of the residual uranium was slowly regained, whilst that of the uranium X decayed. This is most simply explained by the theory that uranium first changes into uranium X. It has been suggested that radium may be the final product of the breaking up of the uranium-atom ; at any rate, it is quite certain that radium must be evolved in some way, as otherwise there would be none in existence—it would all have decomposed. This suggestion has been experimentally confirmed, the growth of radium in large quantities of a solution of purified uranyl nitrate having been observed. Uranium gives no emanation. Thorium probably gives at least three solid products —Meso-thorium, Radio-thorium, and Thorium X, the last of which yields an emanation resembling that obtained from radium, but not identical with it.

§ 93. We must now more fully consider the radium emanation—a substance with more astounding properties than even the radium compounds

Emanation.

themselves. By distilling off the emanation from some radium bromide, and measuring the quantities of heat given off by the emanation and the radium salt respectively, Professors Rutherford and Barnes [9] proved that nearly three-fourths of the total amount of heat given out by a radium salt comes from the minute quantity of emanation that it contains. The amount of energy liberated as heat during the decay of the emanation is enormous; one cubic centimetre liberates about four

[9] E. RUTHERFORD, F.R.S., and H. T. BARNES, D.Sc. : "Heating Effect of the Radium Emanation," *Philosophical Magazine* [6], vol. vii. (1904), pp. 202 *et seq.*

million times as much heat as is obtained by the combustion of an equal volume of hydrogen. Undoubtedly this must indicate some profound change, and one may well ask, What is the ultimate product of the decomposition of the emanation?

§ **94.** It had been observed already that the radioactive minerals on heating give off Helium—a

The Production of Helium from Radium.

gaseous element, characterised by a particular yellow line in its spectrum— and it seemed not unlikely that helium might be the ultimate decomposition product of the emanation. A research to settle this point was undertaken by Sir William Ramsay and Mr. Soddy,[10] and a preliminary experiment having confirmed the above speculation, they carried out further very careful experiments. " The maximum amount of the emanation obtained from 50 milligrams of radium bromide was conveyed by means of oxygen into a U-tube cooled in liquid air, and the latter was then extracted by the pump." The spectrum was observed; it " was apparently a new one, probably that of the emanation itself. . . . After standing from July 17 to 21 the helium spectrum appeared, and the characteristic lines were observed." Sir William Ramsay performed a further experiment with a similar result, in which the radium salt had been first of all heated in a vacuum for some time, proving that the helium obtained could not have been occluded in it; though the fact that the helium spectrum did not immediately appear, in itself

[10] Sir WILLIAM RAMSAY and FREDERICK SODDY: "Experiments in Radioactivity and the Production of Helium from Radium," *Proceedings of the Royal Society of London*, vol. lxxii. (1903), pp. 204 *et seq.*

proves this point. Sir William Ramsay's results were confirmed by further careful experiments by Sir James Dewar and other chemists. It was suggested, therefore, that the α-particle consists of an electrically charged helium-atom, and not only is this view in agreement with the value of the mass of this particle as determined experimentally, but it has been completely demonstrated by Professor Rutherford and Mr. Royds. These chemists performed an experiment in which the emanation from about one-seventh of a gramme of radium was enclosed in a thin-walled tube, through the walls of which the α-particles could pass, but which were impervious to gases. This tube was surrounded by an outer jacket, which was evacuated. After a time the presence of helium in the space between the inner tube and the outer jacket was observed spectroscopically.'' Now, the emanation-atom results from the radium-atom by the expulsion of one α-particle ; and since this latter consists of an electrically charged helium-atom, it follows that the emanation must have an atomic weight of $226\frac{1}{2}-4$, i.e., $222\frac{1}{2}$. This value is in agreement with Sir William Ramsay's determination of the density of the emanation. We may represent the degradation of the radium-atom, therefore, by the following scheme :—

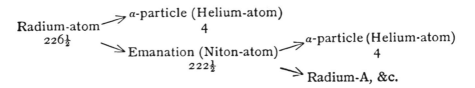

$$
\text{Radium-atom} \; 226\frac{1}{2}
\begin{cases}
\nearrow \; \alpha\text{-particle (Helium-atom)} \quad 4 \\
\searrow \; \text{Emanation (Niton-atom)} \; 222\frac{1}{2}
\begin{cases}
\nearrow \; \alpha\text{-particle (Helium-atom)} \quad 4 \\
\searrow \; \text{Radium-A, \&c.}
\end{cases}
\end{cases}
$$

'' E. RUTHERFORD, F.R.S., and T. ROYDS, M.Sc. : "The Nature of the α-Particle from Radio-active Substances," *Philosophica Magazine* [6], vol. xvii. (1909), pp. 281 *et seq.*

§ **95.** Here, then, for the first time ın the history of Chemistry, we have the undoubted formation of one chemical element from another, for, leaving out of the question the nature of the emanation, there can be no doubt

Nature of this Change.

that radium is a chemical element. This is a point which must be insisted upon, for it has been suggested that radium may be a compound of helium with some unknown element; or, perhaps, a compound of helium with lead, since it has been thought that lead may be one of the end products of the decomposition of radium. The following considerations, however, show this view to be altogether untenable : (i.) All attempts to prepare compounds of helium with other elements have failed. (ii.) Radium possesses all the properties of a chemical element; it has a characteristic spectrum, and falls in that column in the Periodic Table with those elements which it resembles as to its chemical properties. (iii.) The quantity of heat liberated on the decomposition of the emanation is, as we have already indicated, out of all proportion to that obtained even in the most violent chemical reactions ; and (iv.) one very important fact has been observed by some investigators, though it has been denied by others, namely, that the rate of decay of the emanation is unaffected by even extreme changes of temperature, whereas chemical actions are always affected in rate by changes of temperature. It will also be advisable, perhaps, to indicate some of the differences between helium and the emanation. The latter is a heavy gas, condensable to a liquid by liquid air (recently it has been solidified [12]) ; whereas helium

[12] By Ramsay. See *Proc. Chem. Soc.*, vol. xxv. (1909), pp. 82 and 83.

is the lightest of all known gases with the exception
of hydrogen and has been liquefied only by the most
persistent effort.[13] The emanation, moreover, is radioactive, giving off α-particles, whereas helium does not
possess this property.

§ **96.** It has been pointed out, however, that (in a
sense) this change (viz., of emanation into helium) is

**Is this
Change a
true Trans-
mutation?**
not quite what has been meant by the
expression "transmutation of the elements"; for the reason that it is a
spontaneous change; no effort of ours
can bring it about or cause it to cease.[14] But the
fact of the change does go to prove that the chemical
elements are not the discrete units of matter that
they were supposed to be. And since it appears
that all matter is radioactive, although (save in these
exceptional cases) in a very slight degree,[15] we here
have evidence of a process of evolution at work
among the chemical elements. The chemical elements
are not permanent; they are all undergoing change;
and the common elements merely mark those points
where the rate of the evolutionary process is at its
slowest. (See also §§ 78 and 83.) Thus, the essential truth in the old alchemistic doctrine of the growth
of metals is vindicated, for the metals do grow in the
womb of Nature, although the process may be far

[13] By Professor Onnes. See *Chemical News*, vol. xcviii. p. 37
(July 24, 1908).
[14] See Professor H. C. JONES: *The Electrical Nature of Matter
and Radioactivity* (1906), pp. 125–126.
[15] It has been definitely proved, for example, that the common
element potassium is radioactive, though very feebly so (it emits
β-rays). It is also interesting to note that many common substances
emit corpuscles at high temperatures.

slower than appears to have been imagined by certain
of the alchemists,[16] and although gold may not be the
end product. As writes Professor Sir W. Tilden :
". . . It appears that modern ideas as to the genesis
of the elements, and hence of all matter, stand in
strong contrast with those which chiefly prevailed
among experimental philosophers from the time of
Newton, and seem to reflect in an altered form the
speculative views of the ancients." ". . . It seems
probable," he adds, "that the chemical elements, and
hence all material substances of which the earth, the
sea, the air, and the host of heavenly bodies are all
composed, resulted from a change, corresponding to
condensation, in something of which we have no
direct and intimate knowledge. Some have imagined
this primal essence of all things to be identical with
the ether of space. As yet we know nothing with
certainty, but it is thought that by means of the spec-
troscope some stages of the operation may be seen in
progress in the nebulæ and stars. . . ."[17] We have

[16] Says Peter Bonus, however, ". . . we know that the generation of metals occupies thousands of years . . . in Nature's
workshop . . ." (see *The New Pearl of Great Price*, Mr. A. E.
Waite's translation, p. 55), and certain others of the alchemists
expressed a similar view.

[17] Sir WILLIAM A. TILDEN: *The Elements : Speculations as to their
Nature and Origin* (1910), pp. 108, 109, 133 and 134. With
regard to Sir William Tilden's remarks, it is very interesting to note
that Swedenborg (who was born when Newton was between forty
and fifty years old) not only differed from that great philosopher on
those very points on which modern scientific philosophy is at
variance with Newton, but, as is now recognised by scientific men,
anticipated many modern discoveries and scientific theories. It
would be a most interesting task to set forth the agreement existing
between Swedenborg's theories and the latest products of scientific

next to consider whether there is any experimental
evidence showing it to be possible (using the phrase-
ology of the alchemists) for man to assist in Nature's
work.

§ 97. As we have already indicated above (§ 93),
the radium emanation contains a vast store of poten-
tial energy, and it was with the idea of

**The Pro-
duction of
Neon from
Emana ion.**
utilising this energy for bringing about
chemical changes that Sir William
Ramsay [18] undertook a research on
the chemical action of this substance—a research
with the most surprising and the most important
results, for the energy contained within the radium
emanation appeared to behave like a veritable
Philosopher's Stone. The first experiments were
carried out on distilled water. It had already been
observed that the emanation decomposes water into
its gaseous elements, oxygen and hydrogen, and
that the latter is always produced in excess. These
results were confirmed and the presence of hydrogen
peroxide was detected, explaining the formation of an
excess of hydrogen ; it was also shown that the
emanation brings about the reverse change to some
extent, causing oxygen and hydrogen to unite with the
production of water, until a position of equilibrium is

thought concerning the nature of the physical universe. Such,
however, would lie without the confines of the present work.

[18] Sir WILLIAM RAMSAY: "The Chemical Action of the Radium
Emanation. Pt. I., Action on Distilled Water," *Journal of the
Chemical Society*, vol. xci. (1907), pp. 931 *et seq.* ALEXANDER T.
CAMERON and Sir WILLIAM RAMSAY, *ibid.* "Pt. II., On Solutions
containing Copper, and Lead, and on Water," *ibid.* pp. 1593 *et seq.*
"Pt. III., On Water and Certain Gases," *ibid.* vol. xciii. (1908),
pp. 966 *et seq.* "Pt. IV., On Water," *ibid.* pp. 992 *et seq.*

attained.   On examining spectroscopically the gas
obtained by the action of the emanation on water,
after the removal of the ordinary gases, a most surprising result was observed—the gas showed a brilliant
spectrum of neon, accompanied with some faint helium
lines.   A more careful experiment was carried out
later by Sir William Ramsay and Mr. Cameron, in
which a silica bulb was employed instead of glass.
The spectrum of the residual gas after removing
ordinary gases was successfully photographed, and a
large number of the neon lines identified ; helium was
also present.   The presence of neon could not be
explained, in Ramsay's opinion, by leakage of air into
the apparatus, as the percentage of neon in the air is
not sufficiently high, whereas this suggestion might be
put forward in the case of argon.   Moreover, the neon
could not have come from the aluminium of the elec-
trodes (in which it might be thought to have been
occluded), as the sparking tube had been used and
tested before the experiment was carried out.   The
authors conclude : " We must regard the transformation of emanation into neon, in presence of water, as
indisputably proved, and, if a transmutation be defined
as a transformation brought about at will, by change
of conditions, then *this is the first case of transmutation of which conclusive evidence is put forward.*" [19]
However, Professor Rutherford and Mr. Royds have
been unable to confirm this result.   They describe [20]
attempts to obtain neon by the action of emanation

[19] *Journal of the Chemical Society*, vol. xciii. (1908), p. 997.
[20] E. RUTHERFORD, F.R.S., and T. ROYDS, M.Sc. : " The Action
of Radium Emanation on Water," *Philosophical Magazine* [6],
vol. xvi. (1908), pp. 812 *et seq.*

on water. Out of five experiments no neon was
obtained, save in one case in which a small air leak
was discovered ; and, since the authors find that very
minute quantities of this gas are sufficient to give a
clearly visible spectrum, they conclude that Ramsay's
positive results are due, after all, to leakage of air into
the apparatus. But if this explanation be accepted it
is difficult to understand why the presence of neon
should be observed in the experiments with water,
and argon in the experiments with copper solutions
(see below, § 98). We are inclined, therefore, to
accept Sir William Ramsay's results, but it is quite
evident that further experiments are necessary to
settle the question indisputably.

§ 98. The fact that an excess of hydrogen was produced when water was decomposed by the emanation
suggested to Sir William Ramsay and
Mr Cameron that if a solution of a
metallic salt was employed in place of
pure water, the free metal might be
obtained. These "modern alchemists," therefore,
proceeded to investigate the action of radium emanation on solutions of copper and lead salts, and again
apparently effected transmutations. They found on
removing the copper from a solution of a copper-salt
which had been subjected to the action of the emanation, and spectroscopically examining the residue, that
a considerable quantity of sodium was present, together
with traces of lithium ; and the gas evolved in the
case of a solution of copper nitrate contained, along
with much nitric oxide and a little nitrogen, argon
(which was detected spectroscopically), but no helium.
It certainly seemed like a dual transformation of

*Ramsay's
Experiments
on Copper.*

copper into lithium and sodium, and emanation into argon. They also observed that apparently carbon-dioxide is continually evolved from an acid solution of thorium nitrate (see below, § 100). It is worth while noticing that helium, neon and argon occur in the same column in the Periodic Table with emanation; lithium and sodium with copper, and carbon with thorium; in each case the elements produced being of lighter atomic weight than those decomposed.[21] The authors make the following suggestions: " (1) That helium and the α-particle are not identical; (2) that helium results from the 'degradation' of the large molecule of emanation by its bombardment with α-particles; (3) that this 'degradation,' when the emanation is alone or mixed with oxygen and hydrogen, results in the lowest member of the inactive series, namely, helium; (4) that if particles of greater mass than hydrogen or oxygen are associated with the emanation, namely, liquid water, then the 'degradation' of the emanation is less complete, and neon is produced; (5) that when molecules of still greater weight and complexity are present, as is the case when the emanation is dissolved in a solution of copper sulphate, the product of 'degradation' of the emanation is argon. We are inclined to believe too [they say] that (6) the copper also is involved in this process of degradation, and is reduced to the lowest term of its series, namely, lithium; and at the same time, inasmuch as the weight of the residue of alkali, produced when copper nitrate is present, is double that obtained from the blank experiment, or from water alone, the supposition is not excluded that the

[21] See pp. 106, 107.

chief product of the 'degradation' of copper is sodium."[22]

§ **99.** More recently Madame Curie and Mademoiselle Gleditsch [23] have repeated Cameron and

Further Experiments on Radium and Copper.
Ramsay's experiments on copper salts, using, however, platinum apparatus. They failed to detect lithium after the action of the emanation, and think that Cameron and Ramsay's results may be due to the glass vessels employed. Dr. Perman [24] recently investigated the direct action of the emanation on copper and gold, and failed to detect any trace of lithium. The transmutation of copper into lithium, therefore, must be regarded as unproved, but further research is necessary before any conclusive statements can be made on the subject.

§ **100.** In his presidential address to the Chemical

Ramsay's Experiments on Thorium and allied metals.
Society, March 25, 1909, after having brought forward some exceedingly interesting arguments for the possibility of transmutation, Sir William Ramsay described some experiments which he had carried out on

[22] *Journal of the Chemical Society*, vol. xci. (1907), pp. 1605–1606. More recent experiments, however, have proved that the α-particle does consist of an electrically charged helium-atom, and this view is now accepted by Sir William Ramsay, so that the above suggestions must be modified in accordance therewith. (See §§ 89 and 94.)

[23] Madame CURIE and Mademoiselle GLEDITSCH: "Action de l'emanation du radium sur les solutions des sels de cuivre," *Comptes Rendus hebdomadaires des Séances de l'Academie des Sciences*, vol. cxlvii. (1908), pp. 345 *et seq.* (For an English translation of this paper, see *The Chemical News*, vol. xcviii. pp. 157 and 158.)

[24] EDGAR PHILIP PERMAN: "The Direct Action of Radium on Copper and Gold," *Proceedings of the Chemical Society*, vol. xxiv. (1908), p. 214.

thorium and allied elements.[25]   It was found, as we
have already stated (§ 98), that, apparently, carbon-
dioxide was continually evolved from an acid solution
of thorium nitrate, precautions being taken that the
gas was not produced from the grease on the stop-
cock employed, and it also appeared that carbon-
dioxide was produced by the action of radium
emanation on thorium nitrate. The action of
radium emanation on compounds (not containing
carbon) of other members of the carbon group,
namely, silicon, zirconium and lead, was then investigated; in the cases of zirconium nitrate and hydro-
fluosilicic acid, carbon-dioxide was obtained; but in
the case of lead chlorate the amount of carbon dioxide
was quite insignificant. Curiously enough, the per-
chlorate of bismuth, a metal which belongs to the
nitrogen group of elements, also yielded carbon-
dioxide when acted on by emanation. Sir William
Ramsay concludes his discussion of these experiments
as follows: "Such are the facts. No one is better
aware than I how insufficient the proof is. Many
other experiments must be made before it can con-
fidently be asserted that certain elements, when
exposed to 'concentrated energy,' undergo degradation into carbon." Some such confirmatory experiments have already been carried out by Sir William
Ramsay and Mr. Francis L. Usher, who also
describe an experiment with a compound of titanium.
Their results confirm Sir William Ramsay's former
experiments. Carbon-dioxide was obtained in appreciable quantities by the action of emanation on com-

[25] Sir WILLIAM RAMSAY: "Elements and Electrons" *Journal of
the Chemical Society*, vol. xcv. (1909), pp. 624 *et seq.*

pounds of silicon, titanium, zirconium and thorium. In the case of lead, the amount of carbon dioxide obtained was inappreciable.[26]

§ 101. It does not seem unlikely that if it is possible to "degrade" elements, it may be possible to build them up. It has been suggested

The Possibility of Making Gold. that it might be possible to obtain, in this way, gold from silver, since these two elements occur in the same column in the Periodic Table; but the suggestion still awaits experimental confirmation. The question arises, What would be the result if gold could be cheaply produced? That gold is a metal admirably adapted for many purposes, for which its scarcity prevents its use, must be admitted. But the financial chaos which would follow if it were to be cheaply obtained surpasses the ordinary imagination. It is a theme that ought to appeal to a novelist of exceptional imaginative power. However, we need not fear these results, for not only is radium extremely rare, far dearer than gold, and on account of its instability will never be obtained in large quantities, but, judging from the above-described experiments, if, indeed, the radium emanation is the true Philosopher's Stone, the quantity of gold that may be hoped for by its aid is extremely small.

§ 102. A very suggestive argument for the transmutation of the metals was put forward by Professor Henry M. Howe, LL.D., in a paper entitled "Allotropy or Transmutation?" read before the British Association (Section B), Sheffield Meeting, 1910.

[26] For a brief account in English of these later experiments see *The Chemical News*, vol. c. p. 209 (October 29, 1909).

Certain substances are known which, although differing in their physical properties very markedly, behave chemically as if they were one and the same element, giving rise to the same series of compounds. Such substances, of which we may mention diamond, graphite and charcoal (*e.g.*, lampblack)—all of which are known chemically as "carbon"—or, to take another example, yellow phosphorus (a yellow, waxy, highly inflammable solid) and red phosphorus (a difficultly-inflammable, dark red substance, probably possessing a minutely crystalline structure), are, moreover, convertible one into the other.[27] It has been customary to refer to such substances as different forms or allotropic modifications of the same element, and not to regard them as being different elements. As Professor Howe says, "If after defining 'elements' as substances hitherto indivisible, and different elements as those which differ in at least some one property, and after asserting that the elements cannot be transmuted into each other, we are confronted with the change from diamond into lampblack, and with the facts, first, that each is clearly

The Significance of "Allotropy."

[27] Diamond is transformed into graphite when heated by a powerful electric current between carbon poles, and both diamond and graphite can be indirectly converted into charcoal. The artificial production of the diamond, however, is a more difficult process; but the late Professor Moissan succeeded in effecting it, so far as very small diamonds are concerned, by dissolving charcoal in molten iron or silver and allowing it to crystallise from the solution under high pressure. Graphite was also obtained. Red phosphorus is produced from yellow phosphorus by heating the latter in absence of air. The temperature 240–250° C. is the most suitable; at higher temperatures the reverse change sets in, red phosphorus being converted into yellow phosphorus.

indivisible hitherto and hence an element, and, second, that they differ in every property, we try to escape in a circle by saying that they are not different elements because they do change into each other. In short, we limit the name 'element' to indivisible substances which cannot be transmuted into each other, and we define those which do transmute as *ipso facto* one element, and then we say that the elements cannot be transmuted. Is not this very like saying that, if you call a calf's tail a leg, then a calf has five legs? And if it is just to reply that calling a tail a leg does not make it a leg, is it not equally just to reply that calling two transmutable elements one element does not make them so?

"Is it philosophical to point to the fact that two such transmutable elements yield but a single line of derivatives as proof that they are one element? Is not this rather proof of the readiness, indeed irresistibleness, of their transmutation? Does not this simply mean that the derivativeless element, whenever it enters into combination, inevitably transmutes into its mate which has derivatives?" [28]

According to the atomic theory the differences between what are termed "allotropic modifications" are generally ascribed to differences in the number and arrangement of the atoms constituting the molecules of such "modifications," and not to any differences in the atoms themselves. But we cannot argue that two such "allotropic modifications" or elements which are transmutable into one another

[28] Professor HENRY M. HOWE, LL.D.: "Allotropy or Transmutation." (See *The Chemical News*, vol. cii. pp. 153 and 154, September 23, 1910.)

are one and the same element, because they possess
the same atomic weight, and different elements are
distinguished by different atomic weights ; for the
reason that, in the determination of atomic weights,
derivatives of such bodies are employed ; hence, the
value obtained is the atomic weight of the element
which forms derivatives, from which that of its
derivativeless mate may differ considerably for all
we know to the contrary, if we do, indeed, regard
the atomic weights of the elements as having any
meaning beyond expressing the inertia-ratios in
which they combine one with another.

If we wish to distinguish between two such "allotropic modifications" apart from any theoretical views
concerning the nature and constitution of matter,
we can say that such "modifications" are different
because equal weights of them contain, or are equivalent to, different quantities of energy,[29] since the
change of one "form" to another takes place only
with the evolution or absorption (as the case may be)
of heat.[30]   But, according to modern views regarding the nature of matter, this is the sole fundamental

[29] For a defence of the view that chemical substances may be
regarded as energy-complexes, and that this view is equally as valid
as the older notion of a chemical substance as an inertia-complex,
i.e., as something made up entirely of different units or atoms each
characterised by the possession of a definite and constant weight
at a fixed point on the earth's surface, see an article by the present
writer, entitled "The Claims of Thermochemistry," *Knowledge and
Scientific News*, vol. vii. (New Series), pp. 227 *et seq.* (July, 1910).

[30] In some cases the heat change accompanying the transformation of an element into an "allotropic modication" can be measured
directly.   More frequently, however, it is calculated as the difference
between the quantities of heat obtained when the two "forms"
are converted into one and the same compound.

difference between two different elements—such are
different because equal weights of them contain or
are equivalent to different quantities of energy. The
so-called "allotropic modifications of an element,"
therefore, are just as much different elements as
any other different elements, and the change from
one "modification" to another is a true transmutation of the elements; the only distinction being that
what are called "allotropic modifications of the same
element" differ only slightly in respect of the energy
they contain, and hence are comparatively easy to
convert one into the other, whereas different elements
(so called) differ very greatly from one another in this
respect, whence it is to be concluded that the transmutation of one such element into another will only
be attained by the utilisation of energy in a very
highly concentrated form, such as is evolved simul-
taneously with the spontaneous decomposition of the
radium emanation. That this highly concentrated
form of energy does result in effecting the same
appears to be indicated by Sir William Ramsay's
experiments.

§ **103.** We have shown that modern science indicates the essential truth of alchemistic doctrine, and
Conclusion. our task is ended. We can conclude
in no better way than by quoting
these words of the greatest "modern alchemist":
"If these hypotheses [concerning the possibility
of causing the atoms of ordinary elements to
absorb energy] are just," said Sir William Ramsay
in 1904, "then the transmutations of the elements no longer appears an idle dream. The
philosopher's stone will have been discovered, and

it is not beyond the bounds of possibility that it may lead to that other goal of the philosophers of the dark ages—the *elixir vitæ*. For the action of living cells is also dependent on the nature and direction of the energy which they contain; and who can say that it will be impossible to control their action, when the means of imparting and controlling energy shall have been investigated?"[31] This was said before his remarkable experiments which appear to indicate that he has discovered the Philosopher's Stone; and it is worth noticing how many of the alchemists' obscure descriptions of their Magistery well apply to that marvellous something which we call Energy, the true "First Matter" of the Universe. And of the other problem, the *Elixir Vitæ*, Who knows?

[31] Sir WILLIAM RAMSAY: "Radium and its Products," *Harper's Magazine* (December, 1904), vol. xlix. (European Edition), p. 57.

THE END.

The Gresham Press,
UNWIN BROTHERS, LIMITED,
WOKING AND LONDON.

THIS BOOK IS DUE ON THE LAST DATE
STAMPED BELOW

BOOKS REQUESTED BY ANOTHER BORROWER
ARE SUBJECT TO IMMEDIATE RECALL

LIBRARY, UNIVERSITY OF CALIFORNIA, DAVIS

Book Slip–Series 458

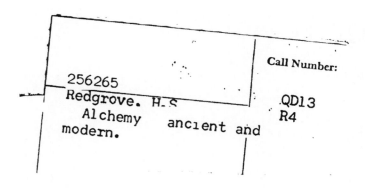

Printed in Great Britain
by Amazon.co.uk, Ltd.,
Marston Gate.